POREDEVIL'S BEAVER TALES

A Double Dozen Mountain Man
Tall Stories Told in Hip-Sprung Verse

EDWARD LOUIS HENRY

D1559836

Christopher
Matthews
Publishing

www.christophermatthewspub.com
Bozeman, Montana

ALSO BY EDWARD LOUIS HENRY

The Temple Buck Quartet
A Rocky Mountain Odyssey

Volume I: Backbone of the World

Volume II: Free Men

Volume III: Shinin' Times!

Volume IV: Glory Days Gone Under

* * *

Poredevil's Beaver Tales

Available from Christopher Matthews Publishing
http://christophermatthewspub.com

Poredevil's Beaver Tales

Cover design by Armen Kojoyian
Lithograph: *The Trappers' Campfire. A Friendly Visitor* by Currier and Ives

ISBN: 978-0-9837225-6-4

Published by
CHRISTOPHER MATTHEWS PUBLISHING
http://christophermatthewspub.com

Bozeman, Montana

Printed in the United States of America

Dedication

For Gloria, without whom nothing would have happened, who never faltered in her faith and loving support; for Kelly, who always believed; and for all the saddle tramps and buckskinners with whom I've been privileged to share a cookfire, swapping lies and trading friendship, throughout my life.

Foreword

This is a collection of mountain man tall stories told in a loose sort of verse. I call it hip-sprung verse; you may call it what you will. In order to understand what these stories are about, imagine yourself sprawled beside a campfire or propped against an aspen tree somewhere in the Rocky Mountains or down along the Arkansas River, sometime in the early eighteen hundreds, listening to a tough mountain man dressed in greasy buckskins spinning highly improbable yarns for the edification — and mystification — of a bunch of greenhorns and a few salty, well-seasoned mountain men like himself — most of the old-timers itching to do him one better with their own whoppers.

Those old-timers weren't really old men. Most of them were in their twenties and thirties, saddle-leather tough and weathered by blazing summers and bone-breaking winters, any weakness they might have carried with them from the settlements long since sweated out or frozen out or scared out in their single-minded quest of beaver pelts — plews, they called 'em.

Why beaver? In the 1820's and '30's, and for more than a century before then, no gentleman in the civilized world considered himself properly dressed unless he sported a top hat made of beaver felt. The men who supplied the beaver pelts were anything but gentlemen. They were a rowdy lot, tough and practical, with enough courage and resourcefulness to match the greed which brought them to the Rocky Mountains from eastern American settlements, Canada, Mexico, Hawaii, and various parts of Europe, with more than a few Delaware and Shawnee Indians thrown in for good measure. It is almost impossible today to imagine the importance and value of beaver fur at that time. Furs were one of the principal exports of the young United States until the late 1830's, when capricious London fashion dictated that the silk hat was in and the traditional beaver topper was definitely old hat. It was just as well, for by that time unrestrained trapping had nearly exterminated the beaver, at least in commercial quantities, from western America.

Mountain men — they mostly called themselves mountaineers — weren't frontiersmen, for they had left the frontier far behind them, east of the Mississippi, and they hoped it would stay there. It didn't, of course, and the glory days of the mountain men lasted a bare twenty years, roughly from 1820 to 1840. But while it lasted, it was a shinin' time for the few who were hardy enough to survive it — a time of hair-raising adventure, in every sense of those words, of rich profits when the trapping was good and the Indians and the elements didn't steal them away, of riotous good-fellowship at the annual fur-trading rendezvous, and, most important of all, a time of freedom for those who were brave enough and tough enough to hang onto it. The free-trapping mountain man wasn't bound by laws or custom, group security, or anything except his individual ability to survive in a harsh natural environment. They were probably the only truly free men in all of history.

In the time of the Rocky Mountain fur trade, the art of the American tall tale probably reached its zenith and has suffered ever since a steady deterioration and declining popularity. Widespread literacy and the subsequent availability of electronic media have eroded the need for people to employ their native creativity to entertain themselves and their companions. It's too easy now to pick up a book or magazine or to dial in our diversions.

For the trappers, however, story-telling developed into a high art. They conjured up impossible yarns lavishly embroidered with digressions and asides calculated to convey an impression of truthfulness. And their solitary occupation gave them ample time to develop some truly outrageous whoppers. The stories presented here seek to recapture and hopefully to perpetuate that swiftly vanishing art.

The language spoken by the mountain men was a casual mixture of French-Canadian, Border Mexican, and a dozen Indian tongues laid on a solid backbone of Appalachian English, corrupted by pride and isolation into a distinctive patois exclusive to themselves. The few among them who wrote anything wrote in the formal American English of their time and no one living today ever heard them speak, so in the following stories you'll hear only echoes of the way I believe they spoke.

Speaking of language, a glossary of terms used during the beaver trade era in the Rockies has been included at the end of this volume. It is no doubt incomplete, but I hope you will find it to be useful.

It's appropriate, too, to mention the treatment of the Blackfoot Indians in these stories. I personally have no quarrel with the Blackfeet — the Siksika, Pikuni, Kainah, and their Atsina allies — but the mountain men did. They feared the Blackfeet more than any other Indians, even more than the Comanches; and because they feared them, they hated them. So what I have to say about the warriors of the Blackfoot Nation in these stories merely seeks to convey the feelings of the mountain men, certainly not my own.

But let's get back to the campfire and listen to their palaver. You'll hear some good stories and maybe you'll get a glimpse of a time when the world was bigger than we have ever known it to be and when some of the men who lived in it were bigger, too.

Poredevil
Edward Louis Henry
Bozeman, Montana

Table of Contents

The Horn

Jim Bridger is perhaps the best-known of all the mountain men. His career as a trapper spanned the years from 1822, when he joined the first fur brigade of William Ashley and Andrew Henry as a lad of 18, through 1840, by which time most of the beaver had been trapped out and London fashion decreed that silk hats and not beaver toppers would be the prevailing style. The beaver trade went bust. Bridger went on to become a trader, an army scout, and a guide and supplier for settlers moving west.

Bridger had several nicknames. The trappers called him Gabe and the Crow Indians named him Casapy, which meant Blanket Chief and wasn't altogether complimentary. Bridger could neither read nor write, possibly because of dyslexia, but he had a keen mind, a prodigious memory, and a tremendous sense of humor; and he had known everybody worth knowing in the mountains. He was a gold mine of tall stories, some his own, some lifted from his friends, just as every good story-teller does. A good yarn, like a good idea, doesn't care where it comes from. It's how you tell it that counts.

The following is a whole pack-string of Jim Bridger whoppers. It's called The Horn.

The Horn

I hear you tenderfoots a-bitchin' an' complainin',
  jist itchin' and a-strainin' to return,
  as rich as yankee gentlemen,
  to settlements along the Mississip.
When will you greenhorns ever learn
  to fasten up your lip an' burn sich memories?
Hearken now, you bacon-eaters,
  r'are back an' take your ease
  an' hear with your own ears
  the kind o' prodigies you'll find
  in yonder shinin' hills,
  if you can hatch the guts an' skills to match
  your greed an' selfish wills.
This Rocky Mountain country's 'bout as big
  an' true as any one o' you
  poor sorry sons o' Satan ever hope to see.
This Rocky Mountain land'll purely shine
  in any company!
Above all places that I roam, I'll claim
  this shinin', untamed home for mine.
Well, it'll surely do for me!
Hell! Hardly any man goes under from
  old age out here!
'Twarn't for grizzly bear and Injuns come
  to raise your hair an' plunder,
and, on occasion, thunderbolts and alkali,
  I swear not one of us would ever die!
Why, anythin'll grow in this here mountain air!
  You see that butte a-shootin' up out there,
  a couple hunnerd yards or so,
  lookin' like an Injun's nose?
Well, hell, there's lots o' those!

That'n, I recall, when Gabe an' me
  come out in fall o' twenty-three
  with Andrew Henry's men.
'Course, the only thing we found
  o' that'ere hill back then
  was jist a measly hole scooped from out the ground.
An' there's the time ol' Bridger chucked a stone
  acrost Sweetwater Crick in twenty-four.
He didn't set no store on it,
    'twas jist a prank, a trick, as you might say.
They call it Independence Rock today!
Waugh! It's jist the way I say!
There's marvels in these mountains
    that's purely past all countin'
    — a mountain made o' magnifyin' glass
    an' boilin' fountains on the Yellerstone
    an' one lone mountain that's
    got rocks that look like trees an' grass.

But strangest thing of all to me,
    takin' ever'thin' together
    — well, for me, it's got to be
    the ever-changin' weather.
Which 'minds me now about jist how
  I learned about the chinook wind
  an' findin' how the weather never stays the same
  an' how Jim Bridger came to get his name.
'Twas in the northern country
  along the way to Hudson's Bay.
As nigh as I can recomember,
    'twas nibblin' on the shank o' late December,
    'long about the year o' twenty-six.
An' cold?! The trees an' sticks a-poppin' in the frost,
  the horses laggin' back an' stoppin',

jist a-holdin' up an' draggin' through the snow,
  an' we was hungry, mostly lost,
  not hardly knowin' where to go.
You'd ne'er believe me if I told
  you jist how cold we was, 'thout even
  any squaws along to keep the sleep robes warm
  an' make you feel you had to act
  like you was brave an' strong.
An' then ol' Bridger come along
  some bodies frozen underneath the snow
  with all their horses, mules an' plews an' plunder
  — a crew o' Nor'west French
  and Englishmen gone under.
We made the best of it, not bein' anybody's fools,
  an' butchered up them Nor'west mules.
An' then we done the best we could
  for all them Britishers an' Frogs
  an' laid 'em out real good an' snug
  beneath some heavy logs.
Then Bridger spied out one o' them,
  an Englishman whose face was calm
  an' peaceful as an infant newly-born
  and in his frozen hand he held in death
  a sort of English huntin' horn,
  lookin' jist like he'd been blowin' on
  that shiny brass cornet
  with his eternal dyin' breath.
Ol' Jim he reckoned that the Englishman
  he didn't need that horn no more
  an' shoved it in his possibles,
  his store o' stuff for tradin' for
  a squaw or p'raps he'd swap it for
  a fine quillwork apishamore.
We made our camp right there upon the snow,

not havin' any better place to go,
  an' tied our stock up to some puny trees,
  so's to keep 'em from the Crees,
  then rolled into our buffler robes
  to sleep like babes until the break o' dawn.
But when at last we come awake we found
  the horses an' the mules was gone
  an' all the trees was mighty bigger all around
  an' more'n somewhat taller, too,
  than they had been the night before.
Ol' Bridger he begun to holler an' to roar
  an' then we heard a neighin' and a brayin'
  an' now an' then a whinny.
Then we looked up an' saw our skinny saddle stock
  a-hangin' by their ropes an' bridle reins up there,
  fair forty feet or more, a-kickin' in the air.
'Twas too high to shinny up an' let 'em to the ground,
  so we jist went an' shot their halter ropes
  to get them mournful critters down.
I reckon that by now you've guessed
  that we'd been blessed by a chinook,
  that warmin' western wind that took
  away the arctic chill an' left as its bequest
  a promise o' the springtime's thrill.
An' then, most marvelous of all,
  we heard a nearby bugle call,
  follered by a stirrin' Scottish air,
  comin' from we knew not where.
The whole brigade we laid about
  to search the unknown bugler out,
  when suddenly the lot of us
  was struck 'most nearly dumb.
The music it was comin' from
  our own Jim Bridger's pack o' goods.

Jim snatched the trumpet from his plunder
  whilst we all watched in awe an' wonder
  — an' then the germ o' truth was born,
  jist like the comin' o' the dawn.
That warm chinook had gone an' thawed
  the music frozen in that horn!

Bridger stuffed a plug o' wood inside o' that cornet
  an' 'lowed 'twas time that we be gettin' on.
But later on the trail, he'd let a little music loose
  to boost us from our robes each day at dawn,
  which is why we call him Gabriel,
  a-trumpetin' like on the Judgment Morn,
  a-playin' wakin' music on that English huntin' horn.
O' course, in time, the music got a trifle thin
  an' warn't no way to store it up agin,
  consid'rin' Bridger had an ear like tin.
So Gabe he traded with an old Shoshone buck
  for a fine paloosie horse
  an' seven pairs o' moccasins
— an' then ol' Jim threw in
his Blackfoot squaw for luck.

'Twarn't the end of it nohow,
  for Gabe somehow he found an echo mountain
  that jist by careful countin' proved to turn
  his voice around an' send it back again
  in jist eight hours lackin' ten.
So whenever we held up an' pitched our camp
  in that hill's neighborhood,
  ol' Bridger stood each night an' yelled,
  "Levez, levez, you sons-o'-bitches,
  roll out them robes an' grab yore britches!"
An' ev'ry morn, jist a mite afore the crack o' dawn,

ol' Bridger's voice comes rollin' back
an' rousts us from our robes,
so's we could pack an' set upon the track
an' get to movin' on.

Now I don't want no arguefyin'
when I tell about the mountain made
o' magnifyin' glass, jist a little north
an' somewhat west o' Jedediah's ol' South Pass.
Crystal pure it is an' lets you see
a wapiti a-grazin' twenty miles away,
lookin' like he'd make an easy rifle shot,
when, fact is, you'd need to ride nigh half a day
to overtake your gazin', like as not.
'Course, you can't exac'ly see that crystal hill,
except by countin' all the wrecks
o' buffler, elk, an' birds that run
into its sides an' break their necks.

Hold on right there!
I'd swear that I jist heard
some bacon-eatin' pilgrim bird
a-laughin' like a loon an' claimin'
all the wonders I've been namin'
are somewhat less than absolutely true!
Well, let me make this deal with you.
When we get up to rendezvous
— if you still think that I'm a liar —
jist spend some time around the fire
an' listen to the talk o' mountain men.
You'll likely hear these tales again.

እ   እ   እ

Peetrified Mountain

One good Jim Bridger story certainly deserves another of the same. Ol' Gabe himself put his brand on a lot of them; and because he lasted longer in the West than just about any other mountain man, still more tall tales were attributed to him, just because he was still around. The next story is one that Bridger almost certainly lifted from Black Harris. It's called Peetrified Mountain.

Peetrified Mountain

I reckon there's a thousand tales
  that men'll tell you 'bout
  the things Jim Bridger's seen an' done.
But here is one that Gabe hisself'll swear
  took place precisely how I'm tellin' you.
Why, you'll be seein' Bridger when
  we all get up to Rendezvous.
Jist ask him then if this here history
  ain't absolutely gospel true.

Now what it is that I've been leadin' to
  is a history as strange an' queer
  as any that you're like to hear.
Seems like ol' Gabe was bringin' his brigade
  a-stringin' down to Rendezvous
  with eighty packs o' beaver made
  in jist the springtime hunt.
The horses was all gant an' Gabe was fed
  to somewhere near to his left ear
  from headin' out in front from can to can't,
  an' so we pitched our camp in a greasy rich
  an' grassy mountain glade an' lazed about,
  turnin' all the mules an' ponies out to graze.
Ol' Gabe he cut hisself a willer pole
  an took some hooks an' went a-fishin'
  down upon a river called the Firehole.
Now, I'll wager my eternal soul and all
  my orn'ry mules an' dearest horses

if that ain't one o' Nature's queerest watercourses!
The water at the bottom's cold as ice,
  whilst at the top it's hot an' fairly bilin'.
You hook your trout down on the bottom, where
  the water's cold enough to freeze your feet,
 but time you haul 'em out through all the bilin' part
  — I truly swear an' cross my heart —
  them fish are cooked an' prime to eat.
About the only place where I could find some fault,
  sometimes they need a trace o' salt.
Well, Gabe he found the fishin' good
  an' he'd et all the trout he could,
  but still he stayed an' laid about
  an' smoked his pipe until
  he reckoned it was long past time
  he'd best be settin' out an' gettin' up the hill.
Ol' Jim was jist a-startin' to
  clinch up his pony's cinch about the time
  he chanced to spy a Blackfoot huntin' bunch
  inchin' down the very hill he meant to climb
  when he went headin' back to camp that night.
He clamped his saddle on real good an' tight
  an' stood a mite o' time a-ponderin' the track
  he'd need to take to shake that Blackfoot scum,
  whose sure intention had to be
  to send him on to Kingdom Come.
Backed up like he was agin the Firehole,
  ol' Bridger lacked a deal o' choices.
He grabbed onto his medicine an' thought
  a time or twice of his eternal soul,
  but naught he done sufficed to bring
  a single one of his own voices near
  — none, at least, that he could hear.
An' then he recollected that there'd been

another butte a-standin' nigh
the mountain top that he hisself selected
an' maybe, jist perhaps,
the two o' them might be connected.
Now ol' Gabe Bridger he ain't slow,
but a hunted man'd better know
jist where it is he aims to go.
Howsomever, Jim he reckoned that he'd wasted time enough
by roughly more'n jist a trifle.
He swung hisself aboard his horse
an' checked the primin' in his rifle,
then galloped off upon a south'ard course,
countin' thirteen Blackfoot bucks
a-foggin' down the mountain,
floggin' on their ponies whilst a-yippin'
and a-yelpin' their Siksika yell,
like all the imps o' Satan comin' out o' hell.
Bridger was a-skirtin' 'long beside
the bottom of that rocky butte,
sartinly not findin' time to rest or even shoot,
an' then he spied a trail a-hidin' 'hind
a curtain o' some queersome kind o' quakin' asp.
Ol' Casapy — the Absarokas call him Blanket Chief —
choked back a gasp o' pure relief
an' plunged his horse on up that track,
most surely runnin' like a thief.
Ol' Jim he hadn't traveled far along
that mountain trail afore he realized
that somethin' thereabouts was dreadful wrong.
First thing that he noticed was
his stirrup brushed agin a bush
and all the leaves begun to shatter.
An' then he spied some antelope that didn't run.
Them critters didn't lope on out an' hide

nor even scatter.
They jist stood like they was carved o' wood,
  a-grazin' or a-gazin' unaware,
  jist as if a rider didn't matter,
  as if they didn't care,
  actin' like he wasn't even there.
'Twas like as if that flock was purely made o' rock.
But Bridger didn't have no time for takin' stock.
Them Injuns they was hard upon his tail,
  nockin' arrows to their bows
  an' closin' up the distance fast,
  their ponies lopin' up the trail,
  and all o' them Siksikas hopin' they'll
collect Jim Bridger's scalp at last.
But as he rode, the sights he saw around him showed
  ol' Gabe this mountain it was surely queer.
The elk an' deer that he saw near
  was standin' in their tracks,
  with here an' there a painter froze
  forever on their backs.
He scraped 'longside an aspen tree
  an' it become a heap o' scree.
Ol' Bridger was plumb mystified
  an' knew this warn't no place to hide
  nor even for to bide some time.
This mountain that he chose to climb
  was absolutely peetrified!

And as Jim Bridger spurred his pony right along,
  some peetrified birds sang peetrified songs
  an' flowers that was peetrified
  was sproutin' here an' there
  with peetrified perfume jist a-hangin' in the air.
The varmints was all petrified

an' didn't even try to hide.
  and all the berries they was precious stones!
An' bein' as not hardly nothin' 'zackly died up there,
  you couldn't even see the customary piles o' bones.
Ol' Bridger never slowed his pace.
He knowed he better win this race
  or face the certainty he'd be
  the guest of honor at a Blackfoot vict'ry dance,
  his hair a-wavin' from
  some heathen Injun's bloody lance.

An' then by Bridger's main intention
  — an' somehat more'n half by chance,
  I likely should refrain to mention —
  ol' Gabe he come upon a cliff
  with no way leadin' down.
His pony he begun to toss his head an' paw the ground
  an' stamp his feet an' champ his bit,
  'cause he could see their nearby camp
  an' he had thoughts o' beddin' down in it.
Ol' Gabe he set a spell an' 'lowed hisself a frown
  an' then he gave his horse a slap an' sez,
  "It's time we move, ol' pard. Giddap!"
Well, truth to tell, that pony looked around at Gabe
  as if he'd gone an' lost his senses,
  but Bridger he jist sets his jaw
  an' then commences spurrin' an' hoorawin'
  out across that yawnin' pit,
  disrespectin' God's an' Nature's ev'ry law
  — an' that's the gospel truth of it!
That pony knew ol' Gabe was boss,
  so he jist hiked his way across,
  a-dancin' and a-prancin',
  jist like a pretty bride romancin' in

her fancy weddin' gown
  — meanwhile avoidin' ever glancin' down.
The distance to the valley floor
  was purely plumb terrific.
The drop from off that mountain top
  was sartinly horrific,
  but Bridger he was scientific.
Well, hell, the simple truth to tell,
  ol' Gabe he knew the gravity
  it was completely peetrified, as well!
Gabe'd nearly made his ride across
  that wide an' peetrified divide
  when all them Injuns galloped up
  upon the other side,
  sartin sure they'd take his hide.
But Jim, by then, was safe in camp amongst his men.
Them superstitious redskins, lackin' Jim's
  specific scientific knowledge
  acquired in the Rocky Mountain College,
  declined to foller out across that holler.
Besides, the odds was suddenly all wrong,
  bein' more'n somewhat long upon the trappers' side.
An' nary Blackfoot that I ever see
  would ride into a fight
  knowin' that the odds was tight.
They like 'em long upon their side,
  like one to thirty-three!
They chose to let ol' Bridger be.
So they got down an' made their camp
  an' 'twarn't hardly any time afore
  each an' ev'ry Blackfoot scamp
  was cripplin' like he had the cramp.
You can see 'em still upon that hill,
  until this very day, I'm thinkin',

away up there upon that mountaintop.
Ev'ry stinkin' one o' them
  bloodthirsty Blackfoot Injuns is
   purely plumb pluperfect peetrified!

                             *   *   *

Snake

Mountain men, much as they might have denied it, were products of the culture from which they sprang. And the white American culture at that time wasn't much given to bathing. Fact is, one of the most unfair things a mountain man could say was to call an Indian a "dirty redskin." That was really a case of the pot calling the kettle black; and the pot was a whole lot blacker than the kettle. Plains Indians of every tribal culture swam or bathed every day if they were able to do so.

Most mountain men truly believed that cleanliness was next to godliness; and they also believed in keeping them both at arm's length. That's pretty much what this story is about. It's called Snake.

Snake

I see you greenhorn would-be mountain men
  a-fightin' shy an' hangin' back
  an' makin' tracks to get upwind o' me
  an' settin' on the other side
  o' this here fire,
  keepin' sich a distance that
  it taxes all the speechifyin' skills
  of even this accomplished liar!
Hell! I know I ain't no violet,
  nor quite some French perfume, an' yet,
  if it warn't for this here smell,
  I reckon I'd be tellin' you this tale
  from someplace in the depths o' hell.
But 'fore I start to give away
  the details o' this history,
  it 'pears to me you oughta know
  the nature an' formation
  of this rancid emanation,
  the slow but sure accumulation
  — addin' jist a mite each day —
  of a beaver trapper's personal bouquet.
Castoreum's the most essential stench,
  the bait we use to drench a beaver set
  to get the critters for their plews.
O' course there's mud an' lots o' blood
  an' grease an' rotgut trader's booze,
  and oozin' from both man an' horse
  a plenitude o' sweat.

An' then, surprises by a grizzly bear
  or Blackfoots come to lift your hair
  contribute more'n somewhat to
  the odor in your britches,
  which is what identifies 'em
  specifically with you.
So, scannin' all the pluses and the minuses,
  the perfume of a mountain man
  is sure to clear your sinuses.

Howsomever, now I'll turn my hand
  to the picture that I aim to draw
  concernin' when I went a-trappin'
  down along the Arkansaw.
That's skinhead Osage land
  an' lately lots o' Cherokee
  uprooted by Ol' Hickory
  from out their home in Tennessee.
Them Injuns didn't fret me none.
After fightin' Piegans, Sioux, an' Ree,
  I reckoned I could do the trick
  with jist a switch o' hick'ry stick.
A mountain man'd hardly need a gun!
  'Course, that's jist a way o' speakin'.
Fact is, my pards an' me was sneakin' through
  that Osage country with uncommon stealth,
  whilst harvestin' a wealth o' beaver plews
  an' thinkin' on the shinin' times they'd buy
  up at the summer rendezvous.
'Twas nigh to spring and ever' livin' thing
  was bustin' to begin its life agin,
  the buds all showin' on the trees
  an' buffler cows a-lowin'.
Plants could hardly keep from growin'.

Wakan-ton-ka promised summer
  on a gentle south'ard breeze.
I was ridin' lazy through the hazy woods,
  musin' on the goods I'd buy at rendezvous
  — an' then perhaps some foofurraw
  for a pert Shoshone squaw
  who chanced to catch my lick'rish eye
  whilst dancin' like a saint in heaven
  up at Bear Lake in twenty-seven.
Wrapped up, I was, in reverie,
  with one more beaver trap to check,
  when somethin' big fell off a tree
  an' landed on my neck,
  then spilled onto my lap.
My horse begun to bolt an 'fore I got a-holt o' him,
  he t'run me to the ground
  — and all around me coils was snappin' tight,
  like coopers fixin' barrel hoops,
  and I was starin' right into the ugly maw
  o' the biggest, meanest blacksnake ever seen
  along the Arkansaw!
At least a rod or two in length he was
  an' thicker than my thigh in girth.
I fought for all that I was worth,
  reachin' for my knife or gun,
  but for all the good I done,
  I could'a been a baby fresh from birth.
Now, blacksnakes they ain't got no pizen,
  but sure as mornin' sun a-risin',
  they'll take your sinful life by squeezin'!
Don't matter the specific reason,
  dyin's hardly ever pleasin',
  'cause what it means to me an' you
  is missin' out on rendezvous

an' losin' next year's trappin' season.
He locked me tight in his embrace,
  his ugly head right up beside my face
  and all his scaly coils a-thrashin'
  in a purely dreadful fashion,
  drawin' taut an' tighter 'til I thought
  my bones'd surely break.
'Twas then I knew the course I had to take.
I realized if I would ever know agin
  life's simple, sinful, carnal pleasures,
  this sitchy-ayshun called for altogether
  desp'rate measures.
I felt my 'tarnal soul a-goin' south,
  so I up an' kissed that sarpint on the mouth!
At first he hissed an' then he gagged.
He missed a wrap or two an' then he jerked
  an' sagged a mite, jist enough for me to work
  my right arm nearly free.
I hated what I had to do, but it was him or me.
He was jist an orn'ry snake
  an' prob'ly didn't mean to make no harm,
  but if that reptile plumb persisted,
  I was sure to buy the farm!
I grabbed his scaly head an' shoved
  it underneath my arm!
What he found in there was mostly hair,
  all matted with a thousand daily sweats
  an' ratted in a pompadour
  with lice who died with no regrets,
  a full methuselah o' scurf,
  an' nigh a peck o' western turf.
'Twas damp an' dank an' ranker than
  a buffler bull in rut
  an' didn't smell no sweeter than

a hydrophoby polecat's butt.
He bucked an' kicked an' started in to fight,
  but all the while he knew he dassn't bite.
Then he begun to cough an' sneeze an' wheeze
  an' purty soon forgot to squeeze.
I gave him still another whiff
  o' that pileous confection
  an' he went stiff an' then begun to shudder,
  sort'a lost direction like a ship
  that's gone an' lost its rudder.
He finally went limp and I kicked free
  an' loosed his head.
He lay unconscious, like he was mostly dead,
  not off'rin' anymore to wrastle,
  jist twitchin' now an' then,
  mebbe thinkin' of a passel
  o' stinkin' mountain men.

I reckoned that I'd gone too far an' felt
  a certain fond regret,
  so I resolved to save his life
  an' keep him for a pet.
I hunkered down an' waited
  until that snake come to.
And when he did, he looked at me
  an' tried to 'scape,
  but that he couldn't do.
He shivered an' he quivered an' then begun to quake.
I reckon that I knew right then
  he was mortal sick, that snake.
He screamed one awful shriek
  an' then he up an' died.
I sighed an' figgered at the least
  I'd take his scaly hide.

I'd have it yet, but fact is,
  I traded it to Cherokees I met up on the ridge.
You can see it still, down on the Arkansaw.
  They use it for a bridge!

                   ৰ   ৰ   ৰ

Jake

Trapping beaver in the Rocky Mountains or farther south along the streams that feed the Arkansas was a hard, dangerous, often lonely occupation. Men became strongly attached to their mules and horses, especially if those animals possessed the qualities of speed, endurance, quickness, judgment, and loyalty. Such a one was a horse called Jake.

Jake

There's some'll tell you that a dog is man's best friend.
Well, I don't know it all, o' course,
  but as for me, I'll send you all
  the dogs there is an' take for mine
  a certain line-back buckskin horse.
I used to call him Jake an' I guess we'd make a pair
  to draw to anytime the goin'
  started in to gettin' rough.
Why, he was tough as smoke-hole buffler hide
  the squaws are fond o' usin' for the winter moccasins.
He never knew the use o' gettin' scared
  an' never spared hisself or me
  or balky pack-mules that he'd nip up near the tail,
  whenever we lined out upon
  a tricky, slipp'ry mountain trail.
Cat-quick he was an' willin'.
Why, he could dance a Texas jig
  upon a shillin', that's a fact,
  burnin' grass beneath his feet
  when he was in the act o' turnin' right about,
  if he should chance to hear
  a hostile Injun shout.
We used to talk a lot, ol' Jake an' me,
  me leanin' up agin an aspen tree,
  him shiftin' legs to ease the cramp,
  when we was wintered in
  at some high mountain beaver camp,
  'way up in the hills, all cold an' dark an' damp,

an' I'd be shavin' off the bark
  o' cottonwoods to give him feed.
I'd need to talk so much, sometimes,
  I taught him all the words I knew
  — an' damned if bein' all alone up there
  didn't force my mind to bend
  enough to comprehend more'n jist a few
  syllables o' horse!

Well, that year, about the time
  the beaver plews was showin' somewhat less'n prime
  an' snow was fallin' light
  an' nights were gettin' shorter,
  we knew that spring was itchin' to begin
  an' we had better orter start
  hitchin' up an' headin' down to rendezvous.
I guess ol' Jake never rightly knew
  what I was frettin' to be gettin' to,
  leastaways not quite at first,
  seein' he was jist a beast,
  but I was surely buildin' one purely monumental thirst.
I baled my plews an' struck my camp
  an' hung my plunder on the mules,
  then swung into the saddle, ready to skedaddle down
  to all the long-neglected pleasures of the rendezvous.
I reckon that I got a trifle careless then,
  as sometimes happens in the spring
  with solitary mountain men.
Why, I could positively taste
  a gurglin' jug of honey mead,
  washin' months o' lonesome from my craw,
  an' feel my hands around the waist
  o' some Shoshone squaw,
  who'd pledge to me, or you,

that she would be forever true
— well, leastaways until the end o' rendezvous.
Even Jake was gettin' lax.
From time to time, he'd take
  his eyes off of the mules an' packs.
I warrant he was tryin' best he could,
  but still that good ol' horse kept eyein'
  that descendin' mountain pass,
  like as if he could already see
  that good, green-growin' valley grass.
Well, whatever caused the trouble
  — an' I'll take a double share for mine —
  ol' Jake an' me we missed a heap of Injun sign.
First thing that we know,
  the trees an' rocks appear to grow
  a hunnerd Injun feathers,
  together with a cloud of arrows buzzin' loud
  enough to be a jillion angry bees.
I grunt somewhat to Jake an' he agrees
  the odds are way too long to stand an' fight.
He switches ends an' then I take
  a narrow pathway to the right,
  yankin' fightin', wild-eyed mules in tow
  an' thankin' all the gods I know
  I'm ridin good ol' Jake.
It's Blackfoots that we come onto
  and I don't mind a-tellin' you
  that we was purely frighted.
From the very moment that I sighted
  all those smoky buckskins an'
  those single eagle feathers in their hair,
  I knew we'd run into a world o' hurt!
And if those Pikunis had their way,
  before this day was halfway done,

ol' Jake an' me'd be eatin' dirt.

The Blackfoots are about
  as mean a bunch o' redskins as ever wore a clout.
Why, they'd rather scalp a white-eyes slow
  even than to kill a herd
  o' buffler or a flock of antelope.
  I hope to tell you so!
Hell, they would rather do without
  than miss a chance o' countin' coup
  on some ol' mountain men
  trappin' beaver on some land
  they happen now an' then to call their own.
Hell, if they'd rest at only countin' coup,
  I'd be glad to let 'em think they're best
  an' get on with the trappin' work
  that I come here to do.
  But no, not them!
Why, in a fight, them Blackfoots
  surely ain't quite right!
Fact is, they're crazier'n a dozen flocks
  o' one-arm wooden clocks!
Only thing that even halfway tamed 'em
  — and it's a sorry shame, I'm thinkin' —
  was the white-eyes' stinkin' pox!
The only time I ever made even halfway friends o' them
  was once when I come up the Muddy from Saint Louie
  with a cage o' cats.
Stole them critters, that's a fact,
  out o' city people's yards!
Made more trade o' them with Kah-ee-nahs
  than I ever made a-playin' dice or hand or cards.
Them Blackfoots sure did prize them cats!
Them kitties kept their tipis from

bein' absolutely plumb overrun with rats!
I reckon that sich favors had purely slipped their mind.
Surely all that they could see, right then,
  was jist another bad an' orn'ry
  white-eyes mountain man.
Wrapped up in me alone
  was all my beaver-poachin' kind.

'Course, what they might'a had in mind
  was the time we chanced to find 'em dancin' medicine
  an' slipped a dozen ponies off their picket line.
If Marley had'n'a gone an' tripped,
  we'd'a done jist fine.
As it was, the dogs woke up the squaws
  an' they, o' course, broke up the dancin'
  an' soon the braves was all advancin'.
Had'n'a been we fought an' killed a couple-three,
  that'd been the end o' Jake an' me.
  Chrissake! them Piegan ponies brought
  a pretty price, I warrant you,
  down at that summer's rendezvous!
Or, it might'a been about the night
  I dodged into the old chief's lodge
  an' coaxed his youngest wife
  into sharin' blankets out beneath the stars.
Right then she wasn't carin' half a mite
  about my bein' white.
'Course, afterwards I had to send her on,
  but what we had that night, 'til pretty nigh to dawn,
  was a nearly magic thing that she an' me
  would always recollect as spesh'ly ours.

Howsomever, reasons didn't matter much right then.
This wasn't any time for thinkin',

only for the savin' of my stinkin' hide again.
Them braves was purely bent on killin' —
  by Christamighty, yes! An' if I miss my guess,
  then widder women are not willin'!
I cut the pack mules loose
  quicker than the blinkin' of an eye,
  then I was bendin' low an' ridin' at a Piegan
  blockin' up the trail
  an' nockin' up an arrow to his bow.
Ol' Jake plumb knocked that Injun pony on his tail
  an' we was showin arse an' hocks
  afore that Injun even hit the stony ground below.
We go racin' 'round a bend
  an' see a sight I swear would send
  your heart a-plungin' to your knees —
  a score o' Piegans waitin' calm an' ready
  underneath the trees.
"Steady, Jake!" I yelled. "Reverse!"
  An' quicker than a skinner's curse,
  he skidded halfway to a stop
  an' turned hisself acrost my knee.
I swear, in spite o' Nature's laws,
  if only he'd been born with claws
  that pony could'a climbed a tree!
Both sides o' the trail was blocked.
Ol' Jake an' me was locked into a box
  — an' the box was gittin' tighter all the time.
There was naught to do but play the fox
  an' climb up off the trail
  an' try to make it through the trees,
  jumpin' over logs an' dodgin' 'round the trunks
  an' list'nin' to the breeze an' thunks
  of arrows flyin' like the summer hail.
We gained a mite o' distance then an' I begun to hope

we had a couple fathoms remainin' to our rope.
Right then we broke out through the trees
  an' what I saw would freeze the blood
  o' braver men than you an' me
  — three hunnerd feet o' cliff
  an' down below, less water than a mare can pee!
Three hunnerd feet — now that ain't much
  — a measly twenty rod, five chain,
  a hunnerd stinkin' yards an' such.
But fallin' off a cliff'll break your neck,
  as like as not.
No matter what you use to measure,
  a drop like that'n spells the end
  of all your earthly pleasure.
The bells was tollin' knells for Jake an' me.
There surely was no place for us to go.
Them Pikunis they was closin' in,
  the old chief leadin' all the band.
I check the primin' o' the rifle in my hand
  an' aimed to blow the gizzard from
  that mean ol' Piegan cuckold
  an' send him off to Kingdom Come.
The powder fizzles in the pan
  jist long enough to spoil my aim
  an' send his right-hand man
  out along the Wolf Trail, whence he came.
I look to Jake, he nods his head.
We know that hangin' 'round
  means surely that we're dead.
Stayin' certifies our dyin' slow,
  so we jump off that cliff an' go
  sailin' toward that sorry little crick below.
Three hunnerd feet ain't much.
  It's over 'fore it fair begins.

Ain't time for Christian folk to tell their sins.
So, "Whoa, Jake!" I yelled.
An' quicker than a hungry parson's benediction,
  I feel the very air a-smokin' blue with friction
  an' Jake a-skiddin' to a stop right there
  — plowin' up a cloud or two,
  I sincerely warrant you —
  an' holdin' in mid-air, a foot or two above
  that cold an' puny shallow crick.
That purely did the trick.
An' then, as purty as you please,
  "Easy, Jake," I said, an' eased us down
  a stitch or two into the water, which
  barely reached that good ol' pony's knees.

This child was laughin' fit to bust,
  thinkin' how them Injuns must be feelin' blue
  at seein' Jake an' me go stealin' off,
  still headin' down to rendezvous.
There's no denyin' I was feelin' sort o' sad
  'bout losin' nearly ever'thin' I had, o' course.
I'd worked two hunnerd days from can to can't,
  gettin' gant an' freezin' arse
  an' sweatin' like a horse
  to trap an' cure them beaver plews.
Still, it wasn't all that bad
  an' there's no use in cryin'.
Hell, how much cash can one man use?
I had my hair an' powder, lead, an' Hawken gun,
  an' most importantly, my horse, ol' Jake.
So what if I had lost a season?
That's no reason to despair.
I could always make another stake.

I wasn't even so partic'lar mad
  at all o' them Pikuni braves.
Bein' proud o' bein' clean-through bad
  was nearly all them heathen redskins mostly had.
There's folks a-growin' up in this here land
  who think the red man is a noble savage an'
  there's others who suppose that he's some sort o' demon,
  a screamin' heathen curse, bent on ravagin' an' shootin',
  takin' scalps an' lootin' an' killin' out o' hand.
Fact is, he's none o' those.
The Injun, he's no better, no, nor worse,
  than any of his white-eyed kin.
It's impossible to tell jist who was first
  to slake his thirst for blood,
  which one was out to save his skin,
  an' who was more than willin'
  that all this killin' should begin.
But my score o' years on this frontier've taught
  smarter men than me that, white or red,
  there's some're fraught with evil, some're good,
  an' lots are better men when they are dead.

I got so busy with my self-congratulatin'
  I plumb forgot this was no time
  for hangin' 'round an' waitin'.
An' then, as if they had the whole thing planned,
  there's painted Injuns standin' all along
  the river bottom sand.
The ones with bows all had 'em nocked
  an' them with trade guns had 'em cocked,
  their painted faces lookin' grim
  or grinnin' with an evil glee, laughin' in anticipation
  o' the dev'lish fun they planned to have with Jake an' me.
Now Lahcotahs ain't so much for torture, an'

Cheyennes are plumb agin it,
  but this hateful Blackfoot lot
  could hardly wait the time when they'd begin it.
They trussed me like a Christmas goose.
It warn't no use a-fightin' to get loose.
They had me dead to rights,
  an' if I had broke free, I solemnly opine,
  they'd'a filled me up with arrows jist like a porkypine.
It warn't half long enough in time
  afore the old chief gallops in like summer thunder,
  follered by a score o' braves a-hazin' up my mules,
  still packin' all my plews an' plunder.
He sets a spell a-gazin'
  with his flinty hate-filled eyes
  an' then by signs an' syllables he makes me realize
  the torture that they planned to do.
They're gonna take ol' Jake
  an' make him into barbecue!

They knew no torture could be worse
  an' I begun to strain an' curse
  an' fight the rawhide thongs —
  an' Jake he whinnies loud an' long,
  jist like a Cheyenne dyin' song.
It took a goodly passel o' them Piegan braves to wrastle
  that good ol' line-back buckskin to the ground,
  but at last they got him down —
  an' jist afore he dies,
  Jake looks at me for one last time,
  pure love a-shinin' from his eyes.
Howsomever, Jake he got a gelding's last revenge.
Once, gettin' mighty nearly loose, he saw to it
  that two or three amongst those braves
  would never make no more papoose.

'Fore long, the meat's a-smokin' on the coals,
  an' all o' them Pikunis jokin' and a-laughin',
  chaffin' me an' actin' like
  an army o' the Devil's own damned souls.
'Bout then, they all commenced to eat,
  crammed their mouths so full o' meat
  they had to work their ugly jaws in utter contradiction
  o' most o' Mother Nature's laws.
  "Whoa, Jake!" I yelled.
The eyes of ev'ry Blackfoot warrior popped.
Ol' Jake jist yanked the brake an' held right there.
  An' when he stopped,
  he choked them heathen redskins fair an' square!

You doubt the truth o' what I'm tellin' you?
Well, hadn'a been for good ol' Jake,
  I'd never seen the way to make it to
  this sorry trappers' rendezvous.

                    ❧   ❧   ❧

Mirage

The next story employs the time-honored saw of "something old, something new." The day that the second caveman managed to stay aboard a horse, horse-racing was invented. Hardly anything swells the pride of a horsebacking man as his being sure that he owns the fastest horse.

There were many things that were new to the mountain men who came to the Rockies and the southern plains and deserts from their homes in the East, Canada, and Europe. The phenomenon which is the subject of this yarn was a new experience for most of them and therefore prime fixin's for the congenial liar who tells his story about a Mirage.

Mirage

I reckon how I've listened to a more'n full sufficiency
  o' reckless talk an' gen'rally unfounded claims
  concernin' certain horses that
  you mountaineers have owned an' seen.
Now grant me time to vent my spleen.
R'are back an' jist prepare yourselves
  to be astounded by this gospel-true recountin'
  of easily the fastest horse there's ever been
  in these here Rocky Mountains.

'Twas jist this spring I'm comin' from
  the Spaniard lands jist north o' Touse
  an' bringin' up my beaver plews
  for tradin' at this rendezvous,
  when I become a mite confused
  about the north'ard trail an' found myself
  in desert land, without no grass or trees,
  much less a waterhole around.
Right now I guess it's best I tell you 'bout
  the horse that I was ridin' on,
  which, I truly must confess, I pilfered from
  a chief amongst the Ute.
Oh, that pony was a beaut!
  A tall an' leggy bay, a horse equipped to run all day,
  short-coupled, with a chest as deep
  as any village well you'll find.
He was gentle as a baby nurse
  an' quicker than a trapper's curse,

with kind an' knowin' eyes.
I named that pony Trapper's Prize.
I called him Prize for short, o' course.
He was the Ute chief's buffler horse,
  but Prize, I sincerely hope to tell,
  could run an antelope to ground, as well.

Well, like I said, no doubt about it,
  we was lost an' starvin', lackin' water,
  trackin' 'crost a sandy waste
  with nothin' but the bitter taste
  of alkali to season up our lips.
I knew that we had better oughter
  find a desert waterhole or we'd be buzzard bait ere long.
The mules was ganted, showin' hips
  to make you think o' knobs for openin' a door,
  laggin' an' jist barely draggin'
  their poor ol' skinny carcasses along.
  Only Prize was goin' strong.
An' then I seen it, way out there, agin the far horizon,
  risin' from the desert like the gates o' Paradise,
  a lake o' water shimmerin', jist a-glimmerin' in the sun,
  surrounded by some tall an' shady trees.
  I scarcely could believe my eyes.
My pony Prize he seen it, too, an' tensed hisself to run.
But then I realized that what I saw jist simply wasn't so.
'Twas nothin' but mirage an' it purely wouldn't do to go
  a-traipsin' after phantoms.
This sartin fact I surely know.
But Prize is jist a beast, a horse,
  an' doesn't know sich scientific things, o' course.
So off he runs an' clamps his teeth upon the bit,
  takin' me along, likin' it or not,
  chasin' that mirage, racin' like a cannon shot.

But that, my companyeros, ain't
  the simple long an' short of it.
'Cause as we come to drawin' nearer,
  I'm damned if things warn't gettin' clearer
  up in that mirage.
There's fish a-jumpin' in the lake
  an' critters, bees, an' birds
  a-flittin' 'twixt the trees,
  and all the fittin' things a body sees
  in natural surroundin's.
But as my pony's feet was poundin'
  and a-drummin' near, that mirage it sees us comin'
  and tries to disappear, drawin' up an' doin'
  ev'rythin' it could to fade.
Jist then that good ol' pony made a mighty leap
  an' landed smack inside o' that mirage
  an' starts a-runnin' back an' forth
  an' to an' fro, nailin' that mirage
  from east to west an' south to north,
  afore it found the time to go.
By time the pack-string trailed on in
  to slake their awful thirst,
  ol' Prize an' me was splashin' in the lake,
  which was that pony's justified reward
  for dashin' in there first.
Then when the stock was watered,
  hobbled, an' set out for grazin',
  I caught some fish an' cooked an' et 'em
  — so tasty you'd not soon forget 'em —
  an' spent the evenin' jist a-lazin' 'round.

Come mornin' light I roused myself
  an' browsed about an' pretty soon I found
  a wealth o' beaver streams surpassin' any trapper's dreams,

containin' a galore an' more o' castors tame as pussy cats.
That's not too much of a surprise, consid'rin' how
  nobody ever trapped 'em in their fairy paradise.
But after I had trapped a couple hunnerd-weight an' more
  o' prime pluperfect beaver plew,
   'twas time, I knew, to close up store
   and amble on to rendezvous.

Now, don't you trappers get to thinkin'
  'bout packin' up an' trav'lin' to
  that stinkin' desert land an' findin' my mirage.
I guarantee that all you'll see
  is nothin' but a heap o' sand.

That final early mornin', jist as day was bornin',
  my pack-string was lined out an' set upon the trail.
I swiveled in the saddle, lookin' 'crost my pony's tail,
  an' saw the trees begin to shrivel
  an' then the grass begun to crumble.
An' next the whole mirage commenced to tumble in.
An' right before my gazin' was a vision most amazin'.
The lake tipped up an' headed for the sky,
  takin' with it all the critters, fish an' fry,
  an' ev'rythin' remainin' was lookin' mighty weird.
Then the whole shebang jist up an' disappeared!

So 'scuse me whilst I wet my whistle.
  My throat's a trifle dry from tellin' you
  this history as straight an' true
  as any gospel or epistle.
  Hold on!
I b'lieve I heard some blunderin'
  benighted pilgrim bird a-wonderin'
  if, in fact, the story that I told was true,

why ain't that horse at rendezvous?

Waugh! Those o' you who know me well will testify,
  the truth to tell, I've got a strong romantic strain
  that sometimes overcomes my brain.
Whilst comin' up to rendezvous
  I run onto a Blackfoot band I've knowed for quite a spell.
Walkin' Eagle is their chief,
  a scoundrelly Pikuni thief,
  who prides hisself on dealin' underhand
  an' practicin' 'most ev'ry sort o' stealth
  for heapin' up a store o' wealth,
  like hardly any Injun that I ever saw,
  in ponies, guns, an' foofurraw.
He an' me been friendly since the night
  the chief fell wounded in a fight
  an', breakin' ev'ry kind o' trapper's law,
  I set my simple mind to spare
  his worthless life an' let him keep his hair,
  which was the only reason
  I was even halfway welcome there.

I wasn't long amongst that band
  afore I saw an Injun lass
  who guaranteed my bachelor days
  were sartin sure to pass,
  if I could only win her hand.
Her name was Pretty Moons,
  ol' Walkin' Eagle's only daughter,
  an' I first seen her stoopin' down,
  scoopin' up some water,
  an' then she smiles and plumb beguiles
  me with some Injun women's wiles her mean ol' dad
  most surely hadn't taught her.

She warn't so much a-comin' forth,
  but, oh, that girl looked mighty sweet
  whenever she was in retreat.
I was hooked as solid as a trout.
  'Twas Pretty Moons that I was sure
  I couldn't live my life without.
I offered Walkin' Eagle all I had
  o' powder, lead, an' foofurraw,
  which would'a been enough an' more
  for almost any Blackfoot squaw —
  but Walkin' Eagle purely had
  his beady, greedy Blackfoot eyes
  plumb fixed upon my fav'rite horse,
  my precious Trapper's Prize.
Well, the final long an' short of it, o' course,
  was, in fact, that thievin' redskin heathen
  swapped me for my truly wond'rous horse
  an' got, in boot, what's more,
  my saddle, bridle, fancy bit, an' porkypine apishamore.
Well, you might think I'd be consumed
  by thoughts of everlastin' gloom,
  but no, I was plumb happified
  by marryin' my Pretty Moons.
She was my blushin' Blackfoot bride
  and I the beamin' groom.

But, sad to say, our honeymoon was terminated way too soon.
Whilst on the way to rendezvous
  — 'twas jist my sorry kind o' luck —
  she run off with a Grovant buck,
  who offered gobs o' foofurraw
  an' thus deprived me of my squaw.

So there you have the whole unvarnished tale

o' Trapper's Prize, the fastest horse
you'll likely ever see amongst
these pale an' shinin' hills.
You can see him still, I dare to say,
  runnin' Blackfoot races
  in all that country up around the way
  o' where the Aitch-Bee-Cee is knowed for keepin' store.

It's more'n likely I should best advise you greenhorns
  to do your walkin' soft an' peel your eyes, up there,
  an' keep your rifle primed an' ready for a fight.
And also, by the way, ye'd best prepare
  by nailin' down your hair real tight.

                        ☙   ☙   ☙

Bear

Mountain men came from a variety of origins and occupations. Many had been farmers; some were sailors or riverboatmen, such as Hugh Glass and Mike Fink. Jim Bridger was an 18-year old apprentice blacksmith when he joined Ashley and Henry's first fur-trapping expedition in 1822; and William Drummond Stewart, although not precisely a fur-trapper, certainly proved himself to be a righteous mountaineer as well as a Scottish nobleman and a decorated veteran of Wellington's Napoleonic campaigns.

Some were fugitives from justice; others, young men of family and education in search of adventure. There were, too, French-Canadian voyageurs and traders, Delaware and Shawnee Indians, Mexican ciboleros, runaway slaves and white apprentices also on the run, and city-dwellers in search of the wealth to be gained from beaver pelts.

No matter who they were, every man who came to the mountains had a lot to learn and those who survived were not particular where they acquired their valuable new knowledge. They were consummate pragmatists who gleaned survival skills from more experienced mountain men, Indians, and even the animals they encountered in the Rockies. They soon learned that, truly, "a good idea don't care where it comes from."

That's the gist of the advice a veteran mountain man gives to a bunch of greenhorn, would-be trappers in the next story. It's called Bear.

Bear

I reckon there ain't hardly any countin'
  all the good an' bad advice
  — pure nonsense an' some commonsense —
  you pilgrims been receivin'
  since leavin' 'hind the settlements
  an' comin' to these mountains.
Beware of ary man who claims to be
  the fountain of all mountain knowledge,
  passin' all his days an' nights
  in talkin' like as if it's he who is
  some special kind o' walkin' Rocky Mountain College.
Nobody knows it all — an' then,
  sometimes the best ideas come
  from some o' Nature's most unlikely men.
Critters, too, contribute to your store o' mountain lore.
Don't matter how or what or who
  delays your trip to Kingdom Come.
A good idea ain't partic'lar
  just where it is it's comin' from.
Which 'minds me of a time when I went huntin' wapiti
  an' finished up by gettin' treed
  an' 'scapin' with my life because
  o' knowledge taught me by a Swede.
'Twas winter on the Yellerstone
  an' we was hunkered down 'til spring,
  too cold for beaver-trappin' or doin' much of anything.
We was perhaps a score o' men
  an' 'mongst us was a Swede,

who'd carried from his native land
   an' clear acrost the eastern oceans
   a pocketful o' downright queersome notions,
   the most o' which I surely didn't need.
Like, he refused to use the Injun snowshoe webs
   that ever'body sees.
Instead he whittled barrel staves
   an' these he called his skis.
O' course, nobody used 'em.
Only some damn fool would think he'd need
   a foreignized contraption suggested by a Swede.

A couple dozen mountain men
   require a galore o' meat an' not a great deal more
   — an' so it fell to me, one snowy winter morn,
   to h'ist myself from out my robes
   an' go perform a huntin' chore.
I put on my snowshoe webs an' buffler coat
   an' checked my powder, ball, an' caps,
   then marched off to the nearby hills
   to bag myself a deer or goat or tender wapiti, perhaps.
I come on up a little rise an' saw a valley down below
   — an' there to greet my gazin' eyes,
   a herd a grazin' wapiti, fair forty elk or more.
Then jist as I was plannin' how
   I'd climb down to the valley floor,
   I heard a loud, blood-freezin' roar
   an' turned to see the silv'ry hide
   o' one plumb angry grizzly boar.
Ol' Ephraim he was shufflin' fast on through the snow.
I snapped a rifle shot an' then
   bethought myself 'twas surely past the time to go.
I'd only nicked his hairy hide
   an' swapped a peck o' trouble for

at least a bushel more.
There surely warn't no time to load
  an' I was blockin' up the road of at least a half a ton
  o' plumb unfriendly grizzly bear.
I shucked my snowshoe webs an' shinnied up
  a tree that was a-standin' there.
But whilst I was so busy climbin',
  I sort'a lost my sense o' timin'.
I saw my rifle slip from out my fumblin' grip
  an' tumble to the snowy ground below.

Now one o' Nature's better laws
  is one concernin' grizzly claws.
They ain't built for climbin' trees.
So if you ever chance to see a bear what's sittin' in a tree
  an' there's a man below, still standin' on the ground,
  you can rest assured the bear's
  black, cinnamon, or brown.
But any time you come to see
  a man who's perched up in a tree,
  while down below there's somethin' awful
  big an' hairy waitin' there,
  I guarantee that you can swear
  that somethin' is a grizzly bear.

Ol' Ephraim had me treed an' that's a fact.
It wouldn'a been for long, except I lacked
  my rifle gun. 'Twas layin' on the ground
  and all that I could do was cuss
  an' trust my pards'd miss me and I would soon be found.

That grizzly bear he was a deal exasperated.
  I reckon he required a final stringy trapper meal
  afore the time that he retired,

hunkered down, an' hivernated.
Ol' Ephraim he was plumb contrary.
At first he strained an' squalled
  an' called me all the dirty names contained
  within a bear's vocabulary,
  crashin' all around the tree an' gashin' up the ground
  — then r'arin' straight upon his hocks
  he'd try to get his claws on me.
I climbed a little higher in the tree,
  increasin' distance from the bear
  an' seein' what was there to see.
On one side was the slope that swept
  down to the valley floor,
  dotted with a double score o' grazin' wapiti.
T'other side contained a puny crick,
  with aspens growin' mighty thick along its rocky shores.
While jist below, Ol' Ephraim roared
  an' bellered grizzly threats an' tore
  at bark with claws that 'peared to be
  at least foot-long or more.
His piggy little eyes they glowed blood-red
  as Satan's evil fire.
His teeth, I could'a swore they growed!
I doubted he would ever tire.
An' then he stopped an' peered at me —
  an' next, he starts a-gazin' at the tree
  — an', 'fore long, I could'a swore
  his crooked little eyes filled up with glee.
He turned an' shambled off, slow an' thoughtful-like,
  pausin' now an' then an' lookin' back at me.
An' then he ambled down to-wards the brook
  an' pretty soon he disappeared behind a tree.

Suddenly I warn't afeared an' reckoned

he had had enough o' playin' at this game.
Whatever was the reason, 'twas all the same to me.
I started havin' thoughts
  o' climbin' down from out that tree.
But jist as I was inchin' to a lower limb,
  I chanced to catch a glimpse o' him
  an' heard a lot o' caterwaulin',
  squallin', and a heap o' splashin'.
An' then I spied Ol' Ephraim dashin'
  back an' forth acrost the crick.
I had no doubt that evil bear had surely fashioned up
  some purely dev'lish hellish trick.
Then, sure enough, he come
  a-crashin' through the quakin' asp,
  surely breakin' Nature's laws.
What I saw fair made me gasp, because
  that bear's a-graspin' on a pair o' beaver in his paws!
He waddles up an' throws them beaver down beside the tree,
  then stands an' looks an' grins at me.
An' whilst I'm wond'rin' what in hell he could be doin',
  he cuffs them beavers mighty smart
  an' starts 'em in to chewin'!
Right then was when I realized
  that bear he was nobody's fool.
'Twas like as if he'd been to school
  an' learned to size up fools like me
  an' pry us loose from out a tree.
He kept them beaver hard at work
  an' batted either one who'd shirk.
They made the chips an' sawdust fly.
I reckoned I was bound to die.
This truly was a time o' need.
'Bout all I had to save my life
  was my Green River skinnin' knife.

Then I recalled our lonesome Swede
  an' how, when we used Injun snowshoe webs,
  he'd whittled barrel staves instead.
That bear intended I'd be dead
  when those damned beaver felled that tree.
  I reckoned I could learn to ski!
My chances they were lookin' slim,
  but there was naught for me to do
  but go to hackin' at a limb,
  then carve an' whittle, trim an' slice
  an' try to make them skis as nice
  an' smooth as any newborn baby's butt,
  while somewheres deep within my gut
  I knew that I was surely runnin' out o' time.
I could nearly hear my fun'ral bells commence to chime.

An' meantime on the ground below
  them beavers never 'peared to tire.
They're gnawin' like a house afire,
  like as if they really know
  that what they got trapped in that tree's
  a beaver-trappin' mountain man.
Them critters hardly never can
  get a beaver's just revenge on such a one as me.

The tree commenced to creak an' totter.
I knew that I had better oughter
  get to gettin' ready for the chance o' my escape.
Then glancin' down I saw that bear
  was fairly dancin' in anticipation
  of a mountain man collation, ugly hairy jaws agape,
  teeth lookin' like a cemetery, grinnin' like a crazy ape.
I cut my buffler coat in strips o' hide
  an' tied my new-made skis on tight,

then clambered out upon a limb upon the downhill side,
  ready as I'd ever be to take my dreadful ride.
Right then I heard the tree stem crack
  an' though I didn't know the use o' skis,
  I knew I'd better get the knack,
  else I would be, most sartinly,
  Ol' Ephraim's mid-day snack.
The tree went crashin' toward the slope
  an' I went shootin' in mid-air an' lit upon my skis,
  thrashin' for my balance, darin' jist a mite to hope
  I'd seen the very last o' that there grizzly bear.
The final sight I had o' him was paws a-wavin' in the air,
  heavin' beavers down the hill, an' shrillin' like an Injun
  that's gone an' lost his hair.
That slope was slick as a gambler's trick.
'Fore long my skis was smokin' hot
  an' I was trav'lin' mile-a-minute, like as not.
I come upon a lodgepole pine
  an' if the choices had been mine,
  I would'a gone to either side.
Instead, I hit that tree astride!
It bent an' broke an' I went on,
  leavin' all its branches gone,
  shootin' off the top an' wishin' that
  I knew a decent way to stop.
As I skedaddled down the line,
  I straddled an' I trimmed
  as many lodgepole pine as you are like to find
  quills upon a porkypine!
Well, at least a double score or more.
  An' I don't mind admittin',
  my upper legs was gittin' sore.
Then I come a-shootin' off a tree
  an' land amidst that herd o' wapiti.

They broke an' ran off from the hill,
  but trav'lin' like I was,
  they could'a been a-standin' still.
Now, wapiti can run real fast,
  but runnin' on those skis I passed
  the cows an' calves an' lit astraddle of
  a big bull elk, landin' like a rock,
  an' broke his neck as neat as if
  I'd hit him with a tomahawk.

I knew 'twas time for takin' stock,
  but what I saw below my belt
  was rather somethin' of a shock.
My clout was gone, my leggin's, too.
The rest o' me was black an' blue.
  An' then I saw that nothin' lacked.
  What counted most was still intact.
I butchered up the wapiti an' packed
  the loins an' hams an' tongue,
  then hustled back along a likely trail to camp.
Lackin' all my nether clothes,
  I minded more'n somewhat the snowy cold an' damp.

The boys was glad to see me, especially with wapiti.
O' course, they laughed an' chaffed me
  'bout bein' naked from the waist.
But what really got 'em wond'rin'
  concernin' my good judgment, not mentionin' good taste,
  an' made them boys to pay some heed
  was when I up an' kissed the Swede.

One final thought on skis'll save
  the most o' you some worry.
I still prefer my snowshoe webs

unless I'm in a hurry.

෧   ෧   ෧

Bill Williams' Dog

Like they say, the first liar doesn't stand a chance and one good fib deserves another. Anybody who ever sat around a campfire swappin' lies knows how it is. No sooner does one man finish spinning a yarn than another one chimes in with one he thinks is even better. This one concerns Bill Williams, who had the reputation during the entire beaver trade era of being the oldest, toughest, greediest, most selfish and contrary mountain man there ever was, either in the Rockies or down along the Arkansas.

This story is told by a trapper who claims to know Bill Williams about as well as anybody ever was allowed to do, although he doesn't seem to be especially proud of it. It's called Bill Williams' Dog.

Bill Williams' Dog

I reckon that there's nothin' wrong
  about a fool who's plumb attached
  to some dumb critter like a horse or dog or mule.
'Tain't breakin' any rule or law.
Why, hell, I knew a trapper once
  who claimed he loved his Blackfoot squaw!
There ain't no shame connected with
  the tamin' of a mule, o' course,
  nor workin' with a saddle horse
  until he's broke plumb gentle.
But as for dogs, I ain't precisely sentimental
  — so for me, I must agree with a custom o' the Sioux.
They raise their dogs to puppy-size
  an' serve 'em up for stew.

Howsomever, what I aim to say in this here history
  concerns Bill Williams an' his dog
  an' how I solved a mystery.
Bill Williams is a lone an' solitary cuss
  and it's jist as well, for he is surely prone
  to raisin' hell an' always one to cause a fuss,
  no matter if it's Injuns he comes up agin
  or them that you'd be callin' his own kind.
He don't never pay no nevermind
  to nothin' don't enrich hisself.
Don't look to Bill to save your bacon.
The only chances he'll be takin'
  will be to build his stock o' plews.

The only men he takes a likin' to
  are jist the men that he can use.
Hear tell he was a parson back in Kaintuck or Tennessee,
  preachin' hell an' brimstone
  an' other forms o' godly arson,
  until he preached his own religion down
  to nothin' but a bitter gall
  an' come out to these mountains
  with no religious faith at all.
You'll see him now an' then,
  but only when he so desires,
  driftin' in beyond the cookin' fires,
  lookin' 'round with shifty eyes as cold an' gray
  as January beaver ponds.
He's old an' long an' lank an' scarecrow slim.
  his rank an' greasy buckskins
  lookin' like they growed on him,
  hunched up like a buzzard,
  his rifle laid acrost his saddlehorn,
  his unshorn thatch o' tangled hair as rusty red
  as on the day that he was born
  — if, in fact, he wasn't hatched!
He's matched by all his animals,
  stringy, lean, an' rawhide-tough,
  none lookin' like they eat enough.

Last time ol' Bill showed up in camp
  'twas nearly winter, cold an' damp.
He come with all his sorry stock,
  a dock-tailed dog a-trailin' on behind,
  a plumb disgrace to all his mongrel race
  — fact is, to all the canine kind.
"Do 'ee hyar?" he cried.
His scratchy voice could shatter glass

an' split a buffler hide in two.
"I've come to catch some beaver plew!
I'll pass a mite o' time with you
  an' pledge I'll let you buy
  my peltries down at rendezvous!"
The booshway warn't too fond o' Bill.
Nobody was. But still, the booshway knew
  him for a trappin' fool,
  though he was cruel an' mean an' stubborn as
  a loco Blackfoot mule.
The booshway sighed an' let him stay
  and, in truth, I'm bound to say
  that all the while Bill Williams stayed,
  that orn'ry cuss most surely made
  three times the beaver plews of any man in our brigade.
We used to call him Solitaire,
  for Bill he always trapped alone,
  declarin' that he wouldn't share
  the things he knew with anyone,
  except perhaps his mangy hound,
  an' no one on this side o' hell
  was ever like to make him tell
  jist how he got his trappin' done.
And ev'ry day he'd harvest a wealth o' beaver plews,
  jist him an' that ol' hound,
  but as regards the methods that he'd use,
  not a soul amongst us ever found.
The queersome thing about it, though,
  was, 'spite of all the plews he'd get,
  ol' Bill would never come in wet,
  nor would his lean ol' dog.
Ev'rybody else in camp
  was shiv'rin' blue an' frightful damp,
  soaked up like a river log an' all stove up with cramp,

with ice upon our leggin's, teeth chatterin' with cold,
  so froze we couldn't hold a cup.
But secrets was a thing Bill Williams never told.
An' if somebody dared to be so bold
  to ask him how they stayed so dry,
  he'd frown an' shrug an' jist shut up
  or say he'd tell 'em nothin', 'cause
  he dast not tell a lie.
Curiosity's what killed the cat, they say,
  an' follerin' ol' Solitaire could surely bring your death,
  but that is purely what I done up there,
  one cold an' wintry late-November day,
  holdin' in my breath an' treadin' soft as any Sioux,
  dreadin' that ol' Bill would hear,
  an' knowin' if he did, exac'ly what he'd do.
Luck belongs to them with pluck
  an' fortune smiled on me that day.
I stalked him like a spike-horn buck.
I follered an' he led the way.
We climbed a ridge or two or three
  an' then one more beyond
  — me hidin' 'hind 'most ev'ry tree —
  afore we found Bill's beaver pond,
  the breeze a-blowin' ripples on the top.
Bill looks around suspicious-like an' tells
  his hungry-lookin' hound to stop.
Then he spies his float-stick ridin'
  out upon the surface o' the pond,
  showin' where his trap is hidin',
  an' when the trap is found, the trap is on a beaver
  and o' course the beaver's drowned.
"Fetch!" says he an' points out to the stick.
The dog ain't dumb an' likely he's come here before.
He jumps onto the pond an' runs out mighty quick,

an' 'fore long, he drug the beaver into shore.

You heard me right! He jumped *onto* that pond!
An' then he *run*, goin' double-quick,
  out to that floatin' stick!
Yes, I'll be damned if I won't wed an' bed
  the Devil's homely eldest daughter
  if Bill's ol' mangy dock-tailed hound
  warn't *walkin'* on the water!
Well, I was absolutely *peetrified!*
I stood straight up an' almost died.
An' dyin's what I nearly done,
  for when I gained my sense once more,
  I'm starin' down the ugly bore
  of ol' Bill Williams' rifle gun.
Howsomever, by that time, nothin' human that I knowed
  could hope to scare me any more,
  so I r'ared back an' then commenced to roar,
  "Shoot if you must, ol' Solitaire,
  do what you think you oughter,
  but tell me jist one single thing
  afore I go to God-knows-where!
Tell me if I saw out there
  your dog *a-walkin'* on the water!"

Ol' Bill he looks plumb mortified,
  embarrassed, like they say.
He heaves a deep an' heartfelt sigh,
  lookin' like he'd like to die,
  an' turns his worn ol' face away.
An' if I hadn't knowed him like I do,
  I'd'a swore his mean old eyes
  was plumb filled up with tears.
"No," says he, "I won't be tellin' you no lies.

I've had that dog for nigh six years,
  through summer suns an' winter snows.
Fact is, I've growed tremenjous fond o' him.
I taught him ever'thin' he knows,
  but damned if I could ever teach
  that gawddamn dog to *swim!*"

                  ঌ   ঌ   ঌ

Bull Elk

Different opinions is what makes horse races, they say, and not everyone in the mountains agreed on the character of Bill Williams. One school of thought believed him to be an unprincipled scamp, while those who claimed to know him best regarded him as a man capable of true friendship, loyal, and dedicated to those few men he regarded as his friends. No one, however, challenged his courage, intelligence, or skills in trapping beaver and staying alive.

Not much is known about Bill Williams' personal life or philosophy, but one trapper claims that Bill told him about the after-life he planned. He tells about it now in a story called Bull Elk.

Bull Elk

Now, there's some'll tell you that they know
  Bill Williams an' they'll try to show
  you jist how mean an' plumb contrary
  ol' Bill can nearly always be.
But what them critters fail to tell
  is jist how very fair an' straight
  that sich a godforsook ol' reprobate like he
  jist about 'most always is
  from time to time can prove to be.
Practical is what he purely is
  an' surely nothin' much gets in the way
  of what he reckons ought to be.
He reckons that by right o' workin' hard an' smart,
  from start o' day 'til dark o' night,
  an' riskin' his own sorrel hide,
  'tain't likely that he'll put aside
  what he decides is rightly his.
Ol' Bill's been in these shinin' hills
  since long before the most of us
  could hardly hold a gun.
And I, for one, have had my fill
  o' greenhorns makin' fun o' Bill,
  'thout knowin' ary aught about
  Miz Williams' orn'ry son.
Bill Williams was a parson in the settlements,
  preachin' hell an' brimstone
  in all o' them revival tents,
  convertin' whites an' Injuns

to follerin' the Jesus trail,
until one day he lost the way
— his faith begun to fail.
An' when he felt it falter,
  he slipped the halter quick an' clean
  an' come out to these mountains
  — set his trail stick headin' west —
  an' traded his religion for Injun medicine,
  'cause, for him, he knew that it was best.

But now I've come up to the part
  where this veracious history should rightly start.
This is jist the way it come about.
You know it must be gospel true,
  'cause you jist seen me cross my heart.

We was layin' up for winter down at Touse,
  the most of us a-hangin' 'round
  a Spaniard bawdy-house.
One night, ol' Bill had nearly drunk his fill,
  when suddenly he turns around an' says to me,
  all solemn-like, jist what he aims to be
  comes time his number's up
  — says when he dies, that he'll return
  a buglin', rutty, ol' bull wapiti.
An' lookin' in his burnin' eyes, I knew
  this warn't no talkin' from a cup.
Ol' Bill was tellin' me no lies.
I realized that what he said he knew was true.
An old bull elk he'd surely be.
An' deep within his flinty eyes, I saw the truth was there,
  an' that, I swear, was good enough for me.
He stared a spell an' then he grins
  'most all the way down to his moccasins,

an' says that elk'll have one lopped-down horn,
so's all his pards'll know
that it's ol' Bill come back to earth reborn
an' mebbe skip a shot an' show
a mountain man's respect for things
the city folk'll never know.

An' now I'll show you how
  Bill Williams surely saved my life.
On that I'll bet my rifle and
  my good Green River skinnin' knife.

'Twas in the fall o' twenty-nine,
  if mem'ry serves me true,
  jist after that year's rendezvous,
  when my Shoshone dad-in-law
  said he knew about a scad o' shinin' beaver plews
  that he was sure'd be comin' prime
  and easily could come to hand about the time
  that I'd commence to trap up in the Absaroka land.
O' course I saw that I would need to leave my squaw
  to winter with her dad's Shoshone band,
  seein's how the Crow delight to lift Shoshone hair,
  plumb out o' hand an' day or night,
  come any time the chance is there.
A white-eyes man don't have that much to fear from Crows.
Those thievin' redskins live to steal
  his horses an' his mules,
  his plunder, plews, an' tack.
So it's not a big surprise they've gone to lettin'
  white-eyes keep their hair, bettin' that us fools
  can't hardly wait to keep on comin' back,
  donatin' to the Crows, ever' bloomin' year.
My squaw she said she didn't mind the waitin',

an', like her kind, she would forgive
my winter fornicatin'
— she said she understood a man must live —
jist so's I didn't take for keeps an Absaroka squaw,
an' come the spring I'd surely bring
prime plews enough to buy for her at rendezvous
great heaps o' foofurraw.

So as early autumn frost was crispin' up the air,
  I lined out my surly pack-string
  an' headed, 'thout a single care,
  acrost the Absarokas,
  to harvest all the beaver waitin' there.
I'd been out a month or more o' time,
  trappin' sich a store o' prime boar beaver that
  I was purely forced to cache four bales o' plews
  — but these, at least, I knew I wouldn't likely lose.
So far I'd kept my hair and all my mules an' horses
  by sneakin' through the trees that hedge
  the banks of all the little watercourses,
  where I was workin' hard an' smart
  an' givin' thanks for dad-in-law's advice,
  an' fightin' 'gin the start o' wintertime,
  when beaver-trappin' halts for snow an' ice.
'Twas late one chilly afternoon an' I was movin' camp,
  an' none too soon, crowdin' on my stock,
  pushin' hard to beat the evenin' cold an' damp,
  comin' through a canyon dark an' narrow,
  when I heard a painter snarlin'
  fit to freeze your marrow.
'Fore I could see 'im through the scrubby trees,
  that devil's darlin' jumps an' knocks
  a packhorse to his knees,
  slashin' and a-gashin' tooth an' claw,

scrapin' him from throat to hocks,
  actin' like he meant to swaller all o' that poor beast
  straight down his filthy maw.
The stock that was a-follerin' set up a fearful hollerin'
  an' turnin' tail, they all stampeded
  back along the canyon trail.
'Course I was I swingin' up my gun,
  but' fore I could take aim,
  my horse begun to r'are an' fell,
  breakin' my right leg to a proper fare-thee-well,
  then scrambled up an' galloped down
   the canyon whence we came.
The last I seen of any beast — o' mine, at least —
  was seein' that poor packhorse struggle to his feet,
  the painter still a-clingin' to his back,
  then lopin' hell-for-leather back down along the track.
I was surely in a sorry plight
  — a busted leg, my horses gone,
  plumb out o' grub, an' winter night a-comin' on.
O' course, I had my knife an' gun,
  a warm capote, a fire-steel
  — but these ain't much to make you feel
  you're likely to be havin' a plenitude o' fun.
By then, the shock o' breakin' bone was wearin' purty thin,
  an' when I tried to move, the pain put out my lights
  — an' I was driftin' home agin,
  liftin' high on crowds o' clouds,
  fadin' into sev'ral thousand darkest nights.

How long I laid there I can't tell,
  but when I woke that broken leg
  was hurtin' so that you'd'a thought
  that ev'ry imp in Satan's hell was bangin' on that bone
  like sextons ringin' on a bell.

But 'spite of all the pain, I found,
  when I awoke, that I was hungrier'n hell.
My belly didn't feel like mine, tryin', like it was,
  to eat a hole plumb through my spine.
I drug myself to water in the crick,
  observin' that for drinkin' it was a mite too thick,
  for plowin', somewhat thin.
  Twas there that I passed out agin.
Next time that I come to, I knew
  that dyin's what I had to do.
Lyin' by that measly crick I realized
  I knew no trick to save my sinful life.
My beaver-trappin' days were through.
I laid there jist a-drowsin',
  watchin' clouds like honeycombs
  massin' up agin the late October sky.
An' then, from out the corner of my eye,
  I spy a big bull elk a-browsin',
  not three rods from where I lie.
Right then I set aside my plans to die.
But jist as I was sightin' down my gun,
  he lifted up his head,
  but didn't make no move to run.
'Twas then I knew that I was jist
  as good as dead an' laid to rest,
  as surely as I knew that I was born.
That old bull wapiti he carried one big lopped-down horn.
I lowered down my rifle,
  sighin' jist a mite, an' more'n jist a trifle sad,
  but sayin' to myself, the primin's likely damp,
  an' cold an' pain'd make my trigger finger cramp,
  an' shootin' layin' on the ground's a sight too rough
  — an' 'sides, a big bull wapiti like him
  is most probably too tough.

But I reckon that I knew jist why I didn't shoot.
I recollected Touse an' what Bill Williams said
  when we was on a trappers' toot,
    about his comin' back agin, after he was dead.
I closed my eyes an' soon I was a-slumberin'.

Next thing I know, I'm joltin' and a-lumberin'
  acrost some craggy ground.
I grit my teeth an' look around
  an' then I found I'm tied onto a travois drag,
  list'nin' to the mournful sound
  of ol' Bill Williams singin' some ol' fun'ral hymn
  'bout bringin' in the sheaves an' such.
Whate'er it were, his singin' wasn't much.

Bill drug me on to Rotten Belly's band, leavin' me up there,
  an' pausin' only long enough to shake my hand
  whilst he was sayin', "Hoss, take care.
These Crows'll do plumb right by you.
I'll see you down at rendezvous."

I reckon that I've seen my fill of Injun medicine,
  what with burnin' purple sage
  an' wavin' turkey feather fans,
  an' screechin' heathen song.
But it wasn't very long until
  they set my leg an' fed an' loved me up
  'til I was perky as a spotted pup.
So much so that when the ice broke up in spring
  I was beaver-trappin' once agin,
  bringin' in a wealth o' beaver plew
  an' dreamin' on the profits I'd make at rendezvous.
And I never even got myself a trifle lathered
  at buyin' back my horses, mules, an' plunder

that them Absarokas gathered.
It was a measly price to pay for all their hospitality.
An' it ain't no wonder that
  — 'spite o' what some others have to say —
  them Absarokas still set mighty well with me.
Come late in spring, 'twas time to go.
  I loaded up my animals an' bade a fond farewell
  to Rotten Belly's Crow.
While on my way I lifted up my cache of autumn plews
  an' then, with somethin' of a heavy heart,
  I left the Absaroka land an' traveled back to see again
  my wife's Shoshone band — then on to rendezvous!

Down at that trappers' rendezvous
  I felt as rich as Jacob Astor,
  after sellin' all my beaver plews an' castor.
But I was only half as happified as my Shoshone squaw
  by time I loaded her with gobs o' foofurraw.
'Twas there I saw Bill Williams,
  sittin' all alone an' drinkin',
  lookin' like he's lost in all the wonder of his thinkin'.
"Thankee, Bill," I says and offers him my kettle,
  jist afore I settle down.
He takes a deep an' healthy draught,
  so deep I thought he'd surely drown.
Then after wipin' off his chin,
  he looks at me an' starts to grin.
"Don't make no nevermind," he says.
"It's what a trapper ought to do."
    An' then,
    "Perhaps I'd best be thankin' you!"

                    ❧ ❧ ❧

Medicine

Mountain men were, most of them, a rowdy, irreverent lot. There were exceptions, of course, such as Jedediah Smith, whose Bible was as important to him as his rifle. But most trappers had abandoned the cant and practice of organized religion along with their need for salt and greens and store-bought clothes. Still, in many of them there was a need to refer to a power beyond themselves. Many of them wore a medicine bag as a good luck talisman and some picked up fragments of Indian religions, imperfectly understood, perhaps, but nonetheless sincerely accepted. A thread of this native faith runs through the following story. It's called Medicine.

Medicine

Injun medicine's a queersome kind o' thing
  for white men's understandin'.
It takes a fearsome heap o' settin at the tipi fire
  gettin' froze for sleep an' keepin' still
  an' tryin' not to yawn,
  handin' 'round the pipe an' list'nin' to
  the red men sing an' smokin' through 'til dawn,
  whilst some old Injun liar pounds a drum an' sings
  an' conjures up the outcome of a buffler hunt
  or perhaps a pony raid an' tells how many head
  they'll bring and if they'll all return,
  or if they won't, how many horse thieves will be dead.
An' it's been known to work for white-eyes jist as well.
Well, hell, as I recall, at rendezvous in thirty-two,
  Jim Bridger gave a brace o' ponies for
  Shoshone medicine when Fitz was more'n somewhat overdue.
The boys all laughed an' chaffed him, but
  the grin slid off their face
  when Broken Hand showed up agin,
  jist like the Injun said he'd do.
I'm 'minded, too, of ol' Levi LeDoux,
  a trapper from Quebec, a French-Canuck who had
  a peck o' trappin', tradin', an' survivin' luck,
  but, problem was, his luck was almost always mostly bad.
Fact is, the sayin' was, at rendezvous, I do recall,
  if it warn't for all the bad luck that he had,
  Levi LeDoux he wouldn'a had no luck at all.
An' then on top of all o' his catastrophes

that flowed on him like some Missourah River,
he was afflicted with the Frenchman's mortal curse
— an' hardly nothin' for a trapper could be worse —
he had the Frenchies' problematic liver.
Now a liver seems to me to be
  the altogether special plunder of Englishmen an' Frogs,
  who 'pear to spend their lives complainin' 'bout
  the fearsome agony an' pain their liver puts 'em under.
So it's no wonder that it's plain for me an' you to see
  that Wakan-ton-ka, Almighty Giver of All Things,
  whether they be sweet or bitter,
  has blessed them foreign critters with a liver,
  an organ that Americans,
  leastaways the ones that I have been about,
  appear to do as well without.
Howsomever, false or true as sich affairs might be,
  Levi LeDoux he passed his days an' nights in misery.
His liver always made him shiver,
  fillin' up his brain with bile,
  grabbin' at him ever' oncet'-awhile
  an' stabbin' him with pain like all the arrows in
  a Blackfoot Injun's quiver.

Well, matters had become so bad for ol' LeDoux
  about the time o' that year's rendezvous
  that Levi purely knew he surely couldn't do
  a trapper's chores no more a-tall,
  come beaver season in the fall,
  which is the only reason that he finally gave in
  an' listened to his Injun wife,
  agreein' that he'd try some Injun medicine.
It'd shut her up an' mebbe let 'im keep his life.
So Levi gathered up a heap o' trade goods plunder
  an' dodged his way on down to Mornin' Thunder's lodge.

Injun medicine don't hardly never come too cheap,
  but after hagglin' some an' Levi bringin' down
  three ponies and another heap o' plunder,
  ol' Mornin' Thunder finally agrees
  to start his singin' an' his drummin'
  an' walkin' out an' talkin' to the trees
  an' callin' on the comin' o' the Spirit
  to chase away LeDoux's disease.

Only Mornin' Thunder knows jist what he did
  to keep LeDoux from goin' under,
  but the wonder of it all was Levi he was fiddle-fit
  come trappin' time in fall.
Levi, why, he felt so good that he was purely shoutin'
  all them ol' French songs an' runnin' wild,
  an' 'fore long his squaw was surely sproutin',
  buffler-big with child.
You could hardly b'lieve the difference it made.
  Levi LeDoux, ever'body knew, was always one to shirk,
  but now he's doin' two men's work
  an' helpin' ev'ry man in his brigade.
There's surely no denyin' Mornin' Thunder
  earned his share o' Levi's plunder
  by keepin' ol' LeDoux from dyin'.
Levi's liver met its match when it come up agin
  a batch o' Mornin' Thunder's medicine.

But 'spite of all his new-found pluck,
  'twas Levi's kind of evil luck
  that fin'ly did ol' Levi in.
What happened happened mighty quick.
Levi didn't have no time for even bein' sick.
He come upon a grizzly sow a-trailin' both her cubs

an' quicker than it takes to shout,
  she r'ares straight up upon her hocks
  an' rubs ol' Levi out.
What was left of ol' LeDoux was mostly widely scattered.
He was, as you might say,
  more'n jist a trifle tattered.
There was barely jist enough remainin' for
  the other boys an' me to carry him
    — exceptin' for his liver,
  which wasn't even hardly sick.
I swear we had to kill that liver with a stick
  afore we could proceed an' go ahead an' bury him!

                              ❧   ❧   ❧

Foofuraw

Mountain men weren't much given to philosophy. They lived too much in the here and now for that. Still, a man who survived in the mountains developed his own set of pragmatic values. He knew what was important to him and what wasn't. But all of us — white man or red or whatever color — carry the scars of early training; and it's well-nigh impossible to get rid of them. About all we can do is to get a clear-eyed look at such notions. The next story is told by a trapper who's got it all figured out, or thinks he has. He knows what is worthwhile and what is just Foofurraw.

Foofuraw

Afore you pilgrims go a-journeyin'
  much farther out upon this prairie trail,
  ye'd all do well to look inside an' ask
  jist what it is you're yearnin' for,
  what took you from the settlements an' made
  you set yourself the hairy task
  o' learnin' this here trapper's trade.
Gettin' rich ain't in it, hoss,
  what with booshway's prices
  — ten or twenty times or more, o' course,
  the cash he paid in some Missourah store —
  an' losin' all your horses, traps, an' plews,
  from time to time,
  to Blackfoots, 'Rapahoes, an' Siouxs.
An' that ain't all, I solemnly declare.
You're jist as apt to lose your hair.

The queersome needs o' humankind I find to be
  consistently amazin'.
For some the spur is buildin' up a name an' fame
  by fearsome deeds o' bravery in war
  or politics that feeds, quite equally,
  upon their brothers' gore,
  while others dedicate their lives to gazin' on
  the pelf collected by their neighbors,
  despisin' what they've got themselves
  an' wantin' more, until
  by knavery an' stealth an' ever-slavin' labors,

they scrimp an' save a mighty store o' wealth,
  jist like as if they didn't know that what awaits
  is jist the grave an' more'n likely nothin' else.
Don't make no consequentiual nevermind
  that most o' folks'll say sich thinkin's fine.
What others say don't make it shine.
I'd jist as lief give up the ghost right now
  as make sich stinkin' values mine.
No, it don't signify jist how
  much fat cow sich doin's 'pear to be.
It seems like mostly nothin'
  but poor bull in rut to me.
Don't matter how you slice it, hoss,
  sich doin's settle crosswise in my craw.
I call it all jist white-eyes foofurraw!

Now foofurraw is what the Frenchies call
  gewgaws an' trinkets, beads an' sich
  that make an Injun woman think she's rich,
  sich plunder as don't really have no worth
  but makes a squaw as proud an' pert
  as any white-eyes queen who walks upon the earth.
Out here a man soon learns to draw the line
  betwixt what's genuwine
  an' what's not worth a tinker's trifle.
First, I hold, is ownin' a plumb-center-shootin' rifle,
  a good Green River skinnin' knife
  that like as not one day'll save your life,
  a warmin' fire when you're cold,
  eatin' when you're hungry,
  drinkin' when you're dry an' hot,
  warm sleepin' robes in wintertime,
  an undiscovered mountain still to climb,
  jist one more prime-condition beaver plew,

meetin' up with friends at rendezvous,
   sharin' good tobacco, drinkin' up a dram or two,
   fleece fat an' roastin' ribs an' buffler hump,
   good horses that can run an' jump a fallen tree,
   an' best of all, jist bein' free,
   not havin' any doin's with the Law.
An' finally, I'm sure you'll all agree,
   the thighs an' sighs an' comfort of an ever-lovin' squaw.
   For me, the rest is foofurraw!

'Twas foofurraw what brung about
   the trouble I'd been glad to do without,
   the very worst catastrophe that ever has occurred to me.
My squaw had lately started in to pout,
   not sayin' much of anythin',
   jist sighin' out each breath she'd draw
   an' dawdlin' over ev'ry chore.
She'd cook the buffler meat to death
   or else she'd serve it mostly raw.
'Twarn't too long afore I come to realize
   she hankered after foofurraw!
We was livin' 'mongst the 'Rapaho, her people,
   an' she loved to show her sisters an' the other squaws
   jist how her white-eyes man'd work his hands
   to callouses an' blisters, providin' her with foofurraw.

'Bout then, a bunch o' young Arapahoes
   was nearly froze to try their hand
   at stealin' horses from a nearby band o' Sioux
   — an' nothin' else, it seemed, would do
   but that I'd go horse-thievin', too.
Well, it was true, 'twas spring
   an' beaver plews were runnin' somewhat thin by then,
   an' still two months to go 'til rendezvous,

so I joined up with nigh a score
o' growin' boys and only somewhat seasoned men
to steal Lahcotah horses, then
to see if we could get 'em home again.
The news o' my departure plumb happified my squaw.
Ere long she was a-countin' up the horses that I'd steal,
jist like as if them ponies was already real,
an' we was hazin' them on down to rendezvous,
— the most amazin' ponies a body ever saw —
— then tradin' all o' them for cloth an' foofurraw.

We started out on foot at night, jist afore the break o' day,
each totin' only what we'd need
to feed along the way an' mebbe fight the Sioux
— a bag o' pemmican, a gun or bow,
a rope, a pipe, a knife or two,
a lad to carry moccasins, an' nothin' more,
exceptin' our own medicine
to save our skins an' help us with
the chore we'd set ourselves to do.
We run due north, two days an' nights,
in mud an' dust an' blazin' sun,
keepin' out o' sight by day an' hidin' from the moon
an' eatin' fast an' snatchin' sleep
an' gettin' up too soon.
An' all the time I'm thinkin',
whilst runnin' down some stinkin' draw,
I'm doin' all o' this
for jist the sake o' foofurraw!
Then we come upon the lodges of a big Lahcotah band,
with spotted horses grazin' jist as far as there was land,
amazin' all the 'Rapahoes,
who clapped a hand upon their mouth,
then chuckled as they planned jist how

they'd drive them stolen ponies south.
They sent a couple-three o' their young men
  around behind the village to decoy the dogs, an' then
  the rest of us crawled out amongst the herd,
  assured we'd have the benefit of all that noise
  to sneak the herd away an' be long gone
  afore the light o' day.
Fact is, in spite of all that well-contrived confusion
  gettin' out alive an' safe was nothin' but illusion.
A young Arapaho, intent on countin' coup,
  run up an' bent his coup-stick half around
  a young Lahcotah herder,
  who picks hisself up off the ground
  a-yellin' bloody murder.
'Twarn't half a blink afore the Sioux
  come bilin' out of ev'ry lodge
  — braves an' squaws an' kids an' dogs —
  like ants a-spillin' out o' half-a-hunnerd rotten logs.
There was nothin' else to do, o' course,
  but grab the nearest Injun horse an' try out-run the Sioux.
The one I caught was big enough,
  a dun with gaits as rough as privy cobs,
  a backbone all composed o' knobs,
  an' birdshot eyes an' Roman nose,
  an' froze to run on his own course.
I truly an' devoutly wish I'd never chose that evil horse!
He had a mouth as tough as saber steel
  an' soon enough it was that I commenced to feel
  he'd pack me 'zackly where it was he wanted to,
  perhaps by chance due south, but more'n likely back
  to his own feedin' grounds amongst the Sioux.
He had a neck as strong as any buffler bull.
No matter how I'd gee an' haw an' tug an' pull,
  he'd lug his head an' move along

like as if I wasn't there, or if I was,
  as if I was already dead.
An' so it was we passed the night,
  a-fightin' back an' forth, me cussin' him,
  until the sun broke out upon the eastern rim.
An' then it was that I looked back
  an' saw a band o' Sioux a-comin' fast upon our track.
He saw 'em, too, an' for once we both agreed —
  bein' 'mongst Lahcotahs was a thing we didn't need.
You'd'a thought he was a centipede!
  the way that horse stampeded out acrost the plain,
  losin' almost all o' them — all o' them but one,
  but on that persistent heathen we simply couldn't gain.
We kept our distance, movin' fast,
  but at last the trail run out
  an' there we had to come about, trapped upon a cliff,
  three hunnerd feet o' nothin' at our back!
But still it wasn't like as if
  that one lone Injun was a pack o' them
  bloodthirsty, sand-inhalin' Sioux
  — an' if I couldn't fight jist one o' them,
  'twas time that I give up the ghost,
  like almost any proper mountaineer should do.
I refilled the primin' in the pan
  an' cocked my Hawken rifle, sittin' tight,
  ready as I'd ever be for one more Injun fight.
The Sioux he charged like prairie thunder
  an' I begun to wonder if his run
  wouldn't sweep us both acrost that bloody cliff.
An' then he slowed an' pulled his pony up,
  a-sittin' straight an' stiff, invitin' me to fight.
'Twas then I swung my rifle up, takin' careful aim,
  and aimin' that I'd make that Injun see eternal night.
His musket was a-comin' up jist when

my horse begun to lunge an' pitch
an' plunge in sich a fashion that
I fired jist a hair too quick,
then saw the flame an' smoke a-flashin',
belchin' thick from out his gun,
an' felt my orn'ry horse a-fallin',
fumblin' for his feet an' stumblin',
holdin' up his head an' bawlin' out
a godforsaken mournful sound,
then slowly foldin' to the ground.
I hit the ground a-runnin' and a-tearin',
 jerkin' out my skinnin' knife an' swearin'
 that I'd sink it to Green River
 in that Lacotah's liver.
His horse, I saw, was slumpin' down,
 the victim of my shot,
 an' the Lahcotah he was jumpin' down an' rollin',
 plannin' how to do me in, as like as not.
He picked hisself up off the ground,
 lookin' mean as painter scut, an' buffler big,
 an' roarin' like an old bull elk in rut.
As I was comin' on to grapple with
 that paint-bedappled Sioux,
 I wondered if that orn'ry horse
 had purely meant to do what surely saved my life
 — an' mostly I decided that he had.
 I reckon that cayuse he wasn't altogether bad.
The Injun he was runnin', too.
I saw he wasn't old an' he was mighty big, even for a Sioux,
 an' when we met he bowled me back at least a rod or two.
We rolled an' hit an' gouged an' bit,
 choppin' and a-slashin', kickin' and a-thrashin',
 throwin' mud made up in part o' blood,
 goin' for the throat an' heart,

an' overlookin' nothin' to assure
the sure extermination of our little part
o' both the white an' redskin nation.
The two of us was bleedin' bad
  from all the bloody wounds we had
  an' slowin' up an' gittin' stiff,
  when suddenly we realized we'd come plumb to the edge
  o' that high an' mighty awful cliff.

We never thought to stop the fight,
  'cause he was red an' I was white.
I saw his knife-hand cocked while we was locked as tight
  as in the close embrace o' love upon that crumblin' ledge.
I looked into his face an' gave one final mighty shove
  an' we went tumblin' off in space.

'Twas foofurraw what done it, like I said.
  That Injun went an' killed me dead.

            ᪥   ᪥   ᪥

Twister

Good advice to any story-teller is to write what you know. Mountain men certainly knew about the vagaries of weather, living as they did, usually unsheltered and exposed to the elements. So it's no surprise that a good many tall stories had to do with capricious weather and how they dealt with it. The next story tells of a tornado and how one trapper put it to good use, or so he says. It's called Twister.

Twister

Hunkered down 'longside o' this here cookin' fire,
  lookin' at your bashful pilgrim faces,
  makes a mountain man like me
  to wonder what it takes to make
  the likes o' you to jump the traces
  an' hire on to ply the trapper's trade.
What made you graybacks leave the farm
  an' put your puny selves in way o' harm?
Why would a counter-jumpin' clerk
  leave his ink-pot, books, an' quill
  to do a beaver-trapper's work?
Which more'n likely's apt to kill the most o' you
  afore you get to rendezvous.
I reckon what the answer is —
  it's nothin' else but pure unvarnished greed!

But if you want to stay alive
  an' mebbe prosper an' survive,
  ye need to listen up an' pay some heed.
Survivin' in the mountains most surely is an art
  an' trappin' beaver plews is only jist a part
  o' what you need to know.
Get smart an' learn the animals
  an' all the plants that grow up here
  an' cultivate some honest fear
  o' rattlesnakes an' grizzly bear
  an' Blackfoots out to take your hair.
'Cause fear's a mighty useful tool.

It makes you quick to act.
The fool who's slow is too soon dead
  an' that's a sartin fact.
Don't trust too much in man nor beast
  an' try, at least, to keep an open mind,
  which more'n once'll help you find
  a way to keep your hide intact.
Which 'minds me now about the weather
  an' how, one time in my career,
  an altogether fearsome wind
  was what I put to use to save
  my sinful, worthless, precious skin.
They say it's gotta be an evil wind that blows no good.
I simply done what any righteous trapper should.

I was comin' up to rendezvous
  from trappin' 'long the Arkansaw,
  dodgin' hostile Injuns like the Kansas, Kiowa, an' Kaw,
  crossin' bare-ass prairies broad an' wide,
  'thout trees or hills or anythin'
  that mebbe could provide a hunted man
  a halfway decent place to hide.
Whilst ridin' 'crost a plain
  an' yankin' on my pack-train mules
  an' thankin' all the gods I know
  for lookin' after fools like me,
  I see a bank o' blue-black clouds a-buildin' in the west.
I reckoned it was best we hunker down
  somewheres amidst that sea o' grass
  until that comin' storm decides to pass,
  'cause even the Almighty God
  can't help a human lightnin' rod.
'Twas then I seen 'em comin' down
  from off a little rise.

I rub my eyes an' realize that what I see
  is a pack o' Grovant Injuns a-headin' straight for me.
Prairie Blackfoots' what they was,
  a bunch o' bucks, without no squaws,
  most likely on their way to make some kind o' war
  or pony raid — God only knows
  what mischief they'd be lookin' for.

Now proper Blackfoots are as bad as Injun bad can be
  — Siksikas, Piegans, Kainahs, they're all the same to me —
  but their Atsina cousins are,
  the sorry truth to tell,
  far worse than Satan's dev'lish imps
  come roarin' out o' hell.
We whupped 'em good in thirty-two
  at Pierre's Hole Rendezvous,
  which didn't help my case right there.
Them Grovants meant to take my hair
  — an' none too quick, I dare to say,
  if them Big-bellies had their way.

I spurred my pinto pony 'round
  as fast as you can blink your eye
  an' yanked my pack-string into line,
  then put the whole shebang into a fine ground-eatin' lope,
  'thout havin' hardly any hope
  I'd do much more than jist delay
  the losin' o' my hair that day.
Them Grovants they was gainin' fast.
  I knew my pinto horse an' mules
  most surely couldn't last until I found a holler or a hill
  where I could halt an' make a stand
  an' send a few Big-bellies to
  their just reward in Promised Land.

Then as we pounded out acrost the plain,
  showin' only arse an' hocks an' tail,
  we run into a spate o' rain, then icy sleet an' rocky hail,
  an' from them ugly blue-black clouds
  there come an awful hummin', whistlin', rumblin' sound
  that fairly shook that prairie ground.
Then partin' through the clouds, my eyes
  beheld a sight that guaranteed
  my sartin trip to Paradise!
Jist a single, solitary look sartinly was all it took
  to leave this sinful trapper mortal shook.
'Twas nothin' else but what they call
  the devil's wind, a prairie twister,
  an' I promise that I'll wed an' bed
  your ugly, eldest spinster sister
  if I didn't surely reckon that I was jist as good as dead.
Them greedy-gutted Grovant Injuns saw it, too,
  but still they kept a-comin' on,
  drummin' 'crost the plain like thunder,
  stickin' jist like cockle-burrs,
  intent to get my scalp an' stock,
  my plunder an' my beaver furs.
There warn't much room to pick an' choose,
  'cause either way I'd likely lose
  my life an' ever'thin' I had,
  so I decided to ride on
  an' take my chance for good or bad.
What happened next took place
  in somethin' less than time it takes to tell.
I spurred my painted pony up
  an' galloped all my wild-eyed mules
  direct into the jaws o' Hell!
Yep, we run into that funnel cloud,
  which proved to be a tunnel leadin' straight

to Satan's evil kind of Eden,
  a turnin', churnin' carousel, a-screamin' loud
  — our destination, surely Hell.
That twister turned me ev'ry way but loose.
  I lost my saddle seat an' reins,
  my rifle, an' my Cayuse horse.
An', o' course, the mules was spinnin' out beyond my reach
  an' now an' then I'd hear 'em snort an' screech,
  but nothin' that I knew to do
  could make no sort o' nevermind.
That kind o' wind is surely boss.
Winnin' jist ain't in it, hoss.
I went whirlin' an' a-twirlin'
  until my hair an' beard was curlin',
  an' then I noticed we was risin'
  slow, but bit by bit, to-wards the top.
An' then I start to realizin' things is slowin' down.
An' though it never slows to what you'd call a stop,
  afterwhile I'm able to stand upright an' almost stable,
  ridin' on the wind, an' the twister never lets me drop.
Then purty soon a horse comes floatin' by.
I think I recognize him by his kind an' knowin' eyes,
  but this critter ain't a paint, he's gray.
An' then I come to realize, o' course,
  the force o' that tornado wind
  has purely skinned the spots away from off my pinto horse.

Well, it warn't too long afore I collected all my mules,
  my rifle, an' my trappin' tools.
Then I noticed we was trav'lin' to an' fro,
  unrav'lin' miles o' countryside,
  where'er that twister chose to go.
I almost was enjoyin' flyin' like a bird,
  when I notice we're approachin' the Grovant pony herd.

I know it's them because I see
  a half-a-dozen horses that was pursuin' me.
The twister comes a-bearin' down
  an' tearin' 'round that pony herd, snappin' up them horses
  jist like a buffler bull a-grazin',
  an' soon I seen 'em raisin' up inside my funnel wind,
  jist as if they're on their way to Heaven.
I gathered all o' them together
  an' put 'em somehow on a tether.
When I was done, I truly swear,
  they tallied up to twenty-seven.
By time I had a chance to look
  that twister's headed for a brook,
  a plumb pluperfect beaver stream,
  an' sucks up all the waters,
  nettin' forty-seven beavers an' a half-a-dozen otters.

'Bout now, my main concern, o' course, is
  how I'm gonna profit from all my new-found wealth
  in beaver plews an' Injun horses,
  a fortune way beyond my countin',
  when I see the twister comin' nigh
  what 'pears to be the Rocky Mountains.
Then as those hills was gettin' near
  enough to see 'em purty clear,
  the twister started turnin' slow
  an' slower, 'til its inner wind fair ceased to blow.
I prayed for all that I was worth
  an' soon we're settlin' down to earth.
That funnel cloud jist up an' crumbled,
  drifted off an' disappeared.
The mules an' ponies, me myself,
  and all my plunder tumbled gently to the ground,
  and all the stock an' ev'ry stick

was absolutely safe an' sound.
I gathered all my plunder an' my plews
  an' loaded up my critters with their packs
  an' then commenced to makin' tracks on up to rendezvous.
Them Injun ponies never gave me any trouble.
Why, you could'a rode them Grovant horses double!
Wind-tamed like them critters was,
  they proved to be as gentle as
  a bunch o' lodge-poled squaws.
They brought a pretty penny, I sincerely warrant you,
  when I sold them ponies off at that year's rendezvous!

If you're lookin' for a lesson in this unvarnished history,
  I truly hope an' pray ye'll find
  it pays to keep an open mind.
So the moral o' this parable
  is no matter jist how terrible
  his current circumstances 'pear to be,
  you can wager ev'ry cent you'll ever see,
  a mountain man'll surely find some way
  to live an' fight another day.
An' you can hear 'em tell it straight an' true
  — jist like I been a-tellin' you —
  next time you see my pards an' me
  up at the summer rendezvous.

                ಶ್ಞ   ಶ್ಞ   ಶ್ಞ

Critters

As I recall, the Scottish poet Robert Burns wrote, "A man's a man for a' that." And never has that sentiment held so true as it did among the mountaineers of the twenties and thirties of the Nineteenth Century. Courage, intelligence, skill, resourcefulness, and fortitude were the only qualities that counted in the beaver-trapping trade. Pride and privilege derived from family or social stratum was baggage best left behind in the settlements before a greenhorn started up the wild Missouri or across the prairies. In the mountains he learned to build his pride upon his own abilities and accomplishments; and if he couldn't do that, he perished.

Such is the experience of the trapper who tells the next story, Critters.

Critters

There's critters in these shinin' hills
  that even Injuns rarely see
  an' white men never guess they're here
  — no, not a solitary one o' them,
  that is to say, exceptin' me.
Them critters are plumb magical
  — heap medicine, as all the Injuns say —
  but to tell about them critters proper
  I need to travel back a way to long before I come out here
  to start a-trappin' beaver plews to make
  some city rake's smart beaver topper.
I wasn't always what you see,
  a mountain man plumb wild an' free
  an' brave an' self-assured an' mountain-smart.
Oh, nosirree! Back at the start
  I was mostly what you see amongst the younger men
  in sleepy towns throughout the South
  — shiftless, down-at-heel, an' mostly mouth,
unlettered, ignorant, an' brash
an' arrogant — what gentlefolk calls trash.
I was loud an' proud an' full o' swagger
  an' if I had a trade 'twas as an empty bragger.
That an' fillin' privies an' gen'rally behavin' bad
  was mostly all the skills I had.
My friends an' me we'd strut on through the town,
  puttin' furriners an' niggers down,
  as if the fact our skins was white

made all our sins an' flaws all right.
One thing I never lacked was pride,
  based strictly on my shade o' hide.
An' then one day I went an' stepped
  somewhat outside the law, jist how far for doin' what
  I ain't prepared to say,
  but far enough to make
  that town an' county way too small,
  so off I run to these here shinin' hills,
  packin' neither cash nor kit, an' knowin' bugger-all.

'Twas Andrew Henry took me up the wide an' wild Missourah,
  forcin' me to pay my dues
  by tendin' camp an' fleshin' plews
  an' haulin' on a cordelle rope
  — an' hopin' to become a mountain man.
But I was mighty slow to learn
  the lessons that you need to earn
  your livin' trappin' beaver plews.
Instead I used my time in criticizin',
  lookin' down my nose an' plumb despisin'
  Delawares an' half-breed French-Canucks
  an' Spaniards up from Touse.
Men who could'a taught me would'a gladly fought me
  for treatin' ever' one o' them
  no better than a gray-back louse.
Whilst Bridger, Fitz, an' mostly all the others
  were learnin' from the redskin brothers
  — trackin', trappin', readin' sign —
  the only counsel that I heeded needed to be only mine.
The wonder of it all is how this child avoided
  goin' under long before my normal time.

An' then one snowy day I found myself

a-trottin' 'long a mountain trail above a deep ravine.
An' though the path was slick as snot an' steep
  as any that I'd ever seen, I paid no nevermind until
  I slipped an' went careenin' down the hill,
    collidin' with some rocks an' boulders,
    skiddin' somehow past the trees,
    first ridin' on my back an' shoulders,
    then rippin' hide plumb off my knees,
    clingin' to my rifle gun an' knowin'
    I'd better find some way o' slowin'
  or I was sartin sure to be some soon-forgotten history.
Right then I purely got my chance.
I landed on the valley floor amid a kind of avalanche.
Last thing that I recall concernin' that tremendous fall
  was one lone rock that bounced agin my head
    — an' as I slipped away into myself,
    I reckoned I was surely dead.

How long I lay there I don't know,
  but when I woke, there warn't no snow
  an', sure as hell, my leg was broke!
Springtime mornin' sun was streamin'
  down upon a medder teemin' with a power
  o' blue an' red an' yeller flowers.
I knew for sure I wasn't dreamin'
  'cause my busted leg near had me screamin',
  all antigodlin twisted like it was
  an' throbbin' with a red-hot pain,
  like Satan's imps an' Blackfoot squaws
  had joined to drive me plumb insane.
Busted up an' all alone an' hurtin' like I was,
  I reckoned life was up for me
    — 'thout contradictin' Nature's laws.
I tried to make my peace an' prayed

the Lord Above my soul to keep
— an' then I must'a drifted off to sleep.

When I come to I saw a slew o' furry little critters standin'
  somewhat less than two foot high,
  with tiny hands an' pointy ears
  an' bright an' beady eyes.
I reached out for my rifle gun, but it was nowheres nigh.
'Twas layin' twenty yards away
  — an' me in no condition to crawl or even try.
An' then those critters picked me up
  — at least a score or more o' them —
  an' toted me onto a grassy mound.
An' when they laid me on the ground,
  they gathered all around an' started in
  to patchin' up my cuts an' scratches
  an' set my busted leg so gentle I didn't even hardly wince
  an' bound it up with strips o' bark an' willer splints.
They built for me a cozy bower
  o' limbs an' leaves an' shady vines
  an' twined with purty garlands made
  of ev'ry kind o' prairie flower.
They brung me gobs o' buffler meat,
  juicy an' all smokin' hot, boudins an' marrow bones,
  an' berries for a treat
  — an' if I'd'a knowed jist what it was,
  caviar, as like as not.
Then after I had et my fill
  to where I was plumb nigh to burstin',
  them critters noticed I was thirstin'.
'Fore long I seen 'em draggin' up
  a kind o' sheep's horn flagon,
  brimmin' full o' sweet metheglin,
  honey mead an' trader's booze

— the kind o' drink a trapper'd choose.
I drank it deep an' long, until
  you'd'a thought I'd get my fill
  — but when I thought I'd have to stop
  an' couldn't hold another drop,
  I'd take jist one more swaller still.

You'd'a thought that all them things
  them little critters did for me
  would surely satisfy their sense o' lovin' charity
  — but no, them critters wasn't finished yet
  with the sorry likes o' me.
They had a heap more plans in store
  'fore settin' this pore trapper free.
As I continued with with my drinkin'
  I couldn't keep myself from thinkin'
  on what it was them critters aimed to do.

'Bout then, one critter standin'
  somewhat taller than the rest
  walks on through his furry crew
  an' amblin' near, he taps me on the chest.
There warn't nothin' much for me to do
  'cept look into his beady eyes
  — an' no matter what I saw in there,
  I swear somehow I knew,
  would prove to be completely true.
Then as I sipped, I slowly slipped into
  a wakin' kind o' dreamin'
  seemin' like the two of us was talkin',
  like trav'lin' in a reverie,
  without no earthly need for walkin'.
Jist how the thing occurred, I ain't equipped to say,
  but somehow, in some magic furry critter way,

he told me that they aimed to heal what troubled me inside,
to peel away my plumb unfounded foolish pride
an' let me see an' feel the real
an' proper goodness underneath my hide.
'Bout then, somewhere deep down, within
  that critter's litle beady eyes,
  I first begun to realize jist what it was that he
  an' all the furry critters wanted me to see
— that who I truly didn't like
  was really no one else but me!
An' then he let me know he knew
  that ever' livin' critter
  needs to think that he's the best,
  like when bull wapitis'll fight,
  provin' to the others that they're better than the rest.
An' afterwhile that critter made me see
  if I had to feel superior, then he an' all his critters
  would be content to be,
  whenever I required, inferior to me.

How long I stayed amongst 'em, I reckon I will never know.
The ever-sweet metheglin never ceased to flow
  from out that sheep's horn cup —
  an' mornin', noon, an' night
  them furry critters served me up
  'most ev'ry kind o' tasty dish
— broiled wapiti an' buffler ribs
  an' sometimes even salmon fish.
But what I got to likin' most,
  even more'n prime roast wapiti,
  was my slowly realizin', comin' on plumb gradually,
  that what I liked the most was me.

An' then one mornin' when I woke

I looked about an' come to see
  there warn't nobody there but me.
My rifle was beside me
  an' my busted leg warn't broke no more.
The whole galore o' critters had up an' disappeared
  an' ever'thin' remainin' commenced to lookin' weird.
'Twas queer enough to make a mortal man afeared.
It begun to seem like ever'thin' had been a dream,
  but when I stooped to pick my rifle up,
  I spied my empty sheep's horn cup.
I'd have that flagon with me still,
  but Paiutes stole my possibles
  when I was trappin' with Ol' Bill.
An' if I ever find which one,
  that's surely one pore thievin',
  unbelievin' heathen that I purely aim to kill.

Then as I left the valley I turned for jist one final look
  an' what I saw fair took my breath away
  an' left me mortal shook.
The flowers was all wiltin' an' a-turnin' brown.
My bower was a-tiltin' an' then completely fallin' down
  — an' snow commenced to fallin' an' a-blowin',
  'til not a solitary thing I knowed was showin'.
I climbed up out o' that ravine
  an' aimed my moccasins to tramp
  a lonesome trail on back to camp.

In camp the boys warn't lettin' on
  they even noticed I'd been gone.
An'if it hadn'a been that I was draggin',
  jist a mite, my lately busted leg
  an' drinkin' from my sheep's horn flagon,
  I might'a got to thinkin' that

some things ain't always what they seem
an' reckoned all of it was jist a dream.
Well, for a change, to make a start,
  I commenced to workin' hard an' smart
  an' helpin' any place where I could lend a hand,
  standin' extry sentry go
  an' roundin' up an' tendin' stock
  an' learnin' from whoever amongst that trapper band.
I learned from big Jim Beckwith
  an' tough ol' Eddard Rose,
  the both o' them plumb hoss enough
  to be adopted by the Crows.
Color surely ain't a gauge o' what a body knows.

The mountains don't have rules an' laws
  you'll find back in the settlements
  an' ev'ry eastern town.
Up here it jist don't signify
  what a man might be back there,
  a gentleman or nigger slave or kicked-out Delaware,
  or black or white or red or brown.
It's handsome-is-as-handsome-does
  an' hoss-what-can-you-do?
An' that, my greenhorn pilgrim friends,
  I found to be plumb gospel true.
An' always somewheres in my mind
  I hung onto this one important thing
  — I'd been elected boss an' somethin' like a king
  of all the furry critter kind,
  so color could become a thing
  to which I paid no nevermind.

I learned the ways o' beaver, deer, an' grizzly bear
  an' how to keep the Blackfoots from takin' off my hair

an' how to keep my powder dry an' ready in the pan.
'Fore long I knew that I could be
  as good or even better than 'most any Rocky Mountain man.
Then after 'while I made a break
  with Ashley's fur brigade an' started in to trappin' free,
  with jist a half-breed French Canuck,
  a kicked-out Delaware, a Spaniard renegade, an' me.
We trapped an' traded ev'rywhere amongst these shinin' hills
  an' clean acrost the plains,
  through summer suns an' winter chills
  an' soakin' springtime rains,
  from Davey Jackson's fav'rite hole,
  clear down the Yellerstone,
  afore we went a-trappin' along the Arkansaw.
An' then a couple winters back
  I took myself a Blackfoot squaw,
  without the measly blessin's of the stinkin' white-eyes law.
So that is how I come to be jist what you see today,
  a bona fide free trapper —
  an' that, you bacon-eaters, is what I aim to stay.

But if the trappin' ever does run out,
  I might contrive somehow to send
  a passel o' them furry little critters back alive,
  so's folks back home'll learn, like me,
  to do some honest thinkin' an' take some worthy pride
  in mebbe somethin' else besides
  their stinkin' lily-colored hides.

          ❧   ❧   ❧

Follower

From 1822, the year General Ashley sent Andrew Henry up the Missouri with his fur-trapping party, most newcomers to the beaver trade began their career in the Rockies by traveling and working with a fur company brigade. Some of those brigades, which operated under a rigid military discipline, numbered as many as two hundred men, occasionally even more. But even with a brigade a man had to be self-reliant. There were no nursemaids in the mountains and self-reliance breeds independence, which makes it hard for some men to take orders. So after a time, when he felt sure of his skills and confident that he could survive the elements and hostile Indians, a man might decide to become a free trapper, working alone or with a few other experienced men and selling his beaver plews to the highest bidder at the annual fur-trading rendezvous.

This story is told by a trapper who recalls just how it was that he abandoned the relative safety of a brigade and struck off on his own to become a free trapper. It's called Follower.

Follower

You ask me how I come to be
  a bona fide free trapper, strictly on my own?
Well, it wasn't always so.
Time was, I traveled with a big brigade,
  makin' my fair share o' beaver hide
  an' gettin' my ideas ready-made,
  takin' booshway's orders, jumpin' when he said to go
  an' pullin' up when he said whoa.
But hard experience has shown
  the likes o' me are better off when hoein' our own row.
I ain't disposed to sit here an' discuss
  all the minuses an' ev'ry plus,
  but I reckon that I'll share with you
  jist how it 'pears to me.
So 'thout relatin' all my history,
  I'll sum it up by tellin' 'bout the time
  I bagged myself a pair o' wapiti.

I calca'late 'twas in the fall o' twenty-four,
  follerin' the Willer Valley Rendezvous,
  an' we was headin' fer Bear Lake,
  when Andrew Henry set our trail sticks pointin' west,
  towards what he said'd let us take
  what was easily the best o' beaver plew
  that we had ever come onto.
He an' Gen'ral Ashley fixed to make a killin',
  so they was more'n willin'

to split our force o' nigh two hunnerd men
  into three brigades o' three-score-odd apiece.
I was purty green back then, o' course,
  an' hardly had the knack o' judgin' horse,
  let alone the worth o' men.
I didn't understand the depth of Henry's skill
  in tradin' with the Injuns, makin' trail,
  runnin' game to earth, evaluatin' horse or mule or men,
  judgin' where to set the camp, an' knowin' when to wait
  an' when to take the trail again,
  or how to judge the weather with an eye
  I vow to you would never fail.
He'd listen, too, a lot.
An' I recall I heard him say to some of us,
  a good idea doesn't care a jot
  jist where it is it's comin' from.
I purely didn't realize the value of his leadership,
  though it was surely there before my eyes.

So when Henry took the middle bunch up north
  an' Jedediah led his train out west,
  we sallied forth — gen'rally a-headin' south —
  follerin' without a single doubtful hunch
  a greenhorn yankee booshway,
  who balanced up his lack o' brain
  with four times more o' mouth.
Now I'll give you all my plunder if soon I didn't wonder
  jist what it was our bosses had in mind
  by choosin' for a leader this greenhorn yankee bleeder,
  this boozin', snoozin' breeder of his mother,
  like no other that you'll find in all mankind.
I later learned this yankee dude
  was shirt-tail kin to Ashley's brood.
He bought hisself a partnership

with money and a lot o' lip
concernin' all their distant fam'ly ties
an' a passel o' some other lies
regardin' God's an' Nature's law.
Indeed I reckon that I know
  what made his arguefyin' stick.
'Twas cold hard cash what turned the trick,
  for greed was always Ashley's fatal flaw.
Nigh seven times a day that booshway'd go an' lose the way
  until we thought he'd lost his mind as well.
They say that you can always tell a yankee, but
  you cannot tell him much. Well, such a man was he.
He'd set the camp where it was damp,
  'til rheumatism gave you cramp,
  or off amidst some rocky scree,
  when eighty yards away there'd be
  a bubblin' brook a-runnin' free.

Contrary's what he was!
Like when we met some Flatheads an' their squaws
  an' he refused 'em 'baccy, beads, an' such.
Them Injuns never asked for much.
We told 'im ever'body knows
  that's what the custom is —
  but he replied, well, mebbe so, but the custom wasn't his.
Result o' that, what happened then, o' course, is
  them Flathead bucks come back that night
  an' stole the mules an' horses.
Discomfort an' Disaster were patron saints o' his'n.
I'd sooner have wet powder lyin' 'neath my frizzen
  than find myself imprisoned 'neath
  the orders an' authority an' rule
  of a fool one-man majority comprised
  o' jist that scandalizin', headstrong yankee mule.

Afoot, with moccasins a-growin' thin,
  we set upon the trail agin,
  luggin' all our plunder on our backs,
  packstraps a-tuggin' on our hide at ev'ry stride,
  hikin' somewheres to the west an' south,
  deprived o' nearly ev'rythin',
  except our everlastin' wonder at
  the booshway's ever-runnin' mouth.
The straw that broke the camel's back
  was runnin' out o' water, the solitary lack o' which
  would make a sane man wed the Devil's daughter
  if she'd show him where he could
  throw hisself into a measly muddy ditch.

Two days we hiked, dried up with thirst,
  an' then the booshway spied it first,
  a pool o' water shinin' out upon the plain!
You'd'a thought we'd gone insane!
Which, in point o' fact, we had.
We bellered like a herd o' buffler bulls gone mad
  an' charged like fools acrost some snowy sand
  around that stinkin' pool, a-drinkin' down our fill,
  never thinkin' that the water might be bad,
  that white an' frosty sand meant alkali,
  and alkali can surely kill.
  Yes, alkali can purely make you die!
Well, it warn't too long afore we realized
  that we were cursed with jist about the worst o' lucks.
We'd slaked our thirst with alkali
  an' ev'ryone come down with flux,
  while only thirty rod from there,
  if we'd only took the time to look,
  spillin' out from 'tween the rocks,
  flowed a pure an' crystal-shinin' brook.

The best o' what come next was mighty bad.
We swore that we'd been hexed.
A score o' men gave up the ghost an' died
  an' most of all the rest was wishin' that they had.
Then purty quick the food run out
  an' then the camp was starvin',
  the men too weak to seek fresh meat.
We're carvin' up our moccasins an' bilin' them to eat.
After time I somehow found the strength
  to crawl as far as my own length an' then a little more —
  oh, jist a measly trifle —
  until there come a day I made it all the way
  outside o' camp, a-leanin' on my rifle.
'Twas only shortly after dawn,
  but somethin' kept a-makin' me keep pushin' on,
  takin' one slow step an' then one more
  — an' then I saw what I was wishin' for,
  a big cow elk, a tender, juicy wapiti
  in excellent condition,
  a packhorse load o' hams an' steaks,
  enough to make my friends an' me
  as healthy as a wealthy English lord
  with all his riches could afford.
That cow was occupied with nothin' else but grazin',
  half-hidden by a boulder, upwind o' me an' gazin'
  only at the grass she meant to crop.
I aimed my rifle 'hind the shoulder,
  leanin' on an aspen for a prop.
I prayed an' aimed an' fired
  an' then, all thanks to God, I seen her drop.

'Bout then was when I sure commenced to ponder
  jist how I meant to tote that elk meat yonder back to camp
  'thout stealin' young Aladdin's magic lamp.

'Twas a wonder that I'd got this far,
  tremblin' weak in both my knees an' peakèd in the arms,
  all in all, as puny as a measly starvin' alley cat.
How was I to haul a wapiti as big as that?
Then somethin' moved. I nearly shat!
I'd gone an' left my powder horn an' ball behind in camp
  and all I had to save my stinkin',
  mortal-sinnin' life was my Green River skinnin' knife.
I waited, watchin', thinkin',
  chokin' back the taste o' fear,
  swearin', if it come to that,
  the price for which I'd sell my life
  would be a cost most ruinously dear.
An' then I see an antler movin'
  somewhere near the bottom o' the rock,
  provin' that I'm suff'rin' from
  some monumental kind o' shock.
No self-respectin' wapiti'd be hangin' 'round
  with it's own relative a-dyin',
  lyin' there an' bleedin' out its life
  upon the cold an' stony ground.
It had to be the Blackfoots, 'Rapaho, or Sioux,
  playin' deadly games, the sense o' which
  I reckon that I'll never know,
  like takin' scalps or countin' coup.
Playin' sittin' duck sure put my nerves on edge,
  so purty soon I crawfished back into the brush,
  anticipatin' any time they'd make a rush.
Afterwards I crawled behind a ledge
  an' circled 'round to get a better look.
What I saw right then fair took my breath away
  — a big bull wapiti, his antlers broad
  as any yankee schooner's sail,
  an' he was bendin' down, his teeth bit hard upon

that cow elk's stubby tail.
I watched some more an' waited,
  hunger gnawin' at my shrinkin' guts the while,
  thinkin' o' me chawin' on that mother elk's big liver,
  flavored with a mite o' bile.
At last I couldn't wait no longer.
May be that big bull wapiti was more'n somewhat stronger
  but he couldn't be no hungrier'n me.
I charged acrost the clearin',
  careerin' like a man what's gone an' lost his mind,
  screamin' Injun yells an' hardly fearin'
  nothin' from that bull as I was nearin' him,
  then slowly realizin' that this stationary wapiti,
  contrary to his breed and kind,
  was purely payin' me no mind!
  This dedicated wapiti was surely blind!
I sidled close upon the downwind side
  to see if I was right. I'd say
  this bull had never seen the light o' day.
Bein' blind from birth, he'd had to trail
  his way acrost the surface o' the earth,
  his teeth clenched down upon his mama's tail!

Hunger'd got the best o' me, I swear!
I'd'a braved a grizzly bear, let alone a wapiti.
I ripped the old cow clean from throat to you-know-where
  an' dove inside, a-pushin' past
  the kidneys, heart, an' spleen,
  headin' for the liver an' the gall
  I knew was waitin' there,
  — an' knowin', later on, I'd eat it all.
His mama's blood had quite destroyed
  the young bull's sense o' smell.
Otherwise, I'd say, he'd'a kicked me plumb to hell!

Afterwards, a-leanin' back
  an' wishin' for some 'baccy an' my pipe
  an' waitin' for my guts to gripe,
  I got to thinkin' how I'd get the meat
  to my companions back at camp,
  when I observed that wapiti
  had never loosed his dreadful clamp upon his mama's tail.
One thought will surely lead you out
  upon the trail of sartinly another.
'Bout then it was that I begun to heed
  the lessons I had learned.
No matter how his circumstances turned,
  first one bad way an' then another,
  that young bull wapiti had spurned
  his native fears an' clung onto the tail
  that hung behind his mother.
'Twas then I realized that I had found the way
  to how I'd pack the meat o' that cow wapiti.
Mountain men like me don't hardly never trust to luck.
It's pluck won't hardly never fail.
So now I jist cut off that tail
  an' quartered up the cow, slicin' off some strips o' hide
  I used to hang her off each side
  o' that young bull, somehow.
He didn't like the smell o' blood, o' course,
  but he stood firm, much like a good but unbroke horse,
  heavin', now an' then, a fearful shudder,
  whilst I was loadin' on his back
  the carcass of his dear departed mother.
Then, gently tuggin' on the old cow's tail,
  I guided him along my homeward trail.

Hikin' back along the track, I sort'a took
  a likin' to that bull, but it was then

that I recalled jist what, in camp,
his sartin fate must be,
when two-score starvin' mountain men
eyeballed this sightless wapiti.
I shook them gentle thoughts clean out o' mind.
This wapiti was jist a beast
  an' they, at least, were my own kind.

Whilst I was amblin' on,
  such random thoughts a-ramblin' in my mind,
  I got to thinkin' how there warn't too much
  that differed 'twixt that wapiti an' me.
Blind he was an' had to suffer bein' led.
Now, purty soon, this critter would be dead.
But how was I so different? Follerin' a fool
  an' jumpin' when he hollered out
  still yet another damnfool rule!
I'd come out to be a mountain man
  an' now I'd come to takin' crumbs
  from some damnyankee's stingy hand!
An' then it was I told myself,
  Hey! I'm the only man amongst this sorry crew
  come bringin' in the meat of elk!
So let the wide blue welkin ring
  the breadth of all this mountain land,
  echoin' the voice o' this here mountain man,
  who's decided once for all to make his final stand!
There's jist one possibility for a mountaineer like me
  an' that is simply bein' free!

'Twas then an' there that I made up my mind
  jist what it was I had to do.
An' if you had knowed the booshway or any of his kind,
  you'd'a done it, too.

Back at camp, 'twas jist about as I had reckoned it'd be.
Men grown gant an' hardly more
  than skin an' bone attacked the wapiti
  an' had his steaks — an' mama's, too —
  sizzlin' on the glowin' coals
  quicker than ol' Satan takes
  to snatch our mortal-sinnin' souls.
I claimed the elk teeth as my prize,
  realizin' that I'd need some goods
  for tradin' with the Crow or mebbe jist to tantalize
  some maiden o' the 'Rapaho.
That night I packed my rifle, traps, an' plunder
  an' sundered all the ties I had
  with booshways an' brigades an' such.
It wasn't hard to carry.
This benighted, blighted expedition
  truly hadn't left us much.

Two days out I chanced upon some Crow
  an' traded off them elk teeth for a horse.
An' after that it warn't too long afore I stole
  a couple more, o' course.

I wintered 'mongst the 'Rapaho,
  shavin' ev'ry day an' savin' ev'ry beaver plew
  an' waitin' for the time when I'd show up
  down at the summer rendezvous.
An' often of a winter night I'd think o' that blind wapiti
  an' how he had to foller on behind his mother,
  his life an' livelihood dependent on another.
'Twas times like that I surely knew,
  no matter what my fate might be,
  I'd never ever foller anyone but me!

The Jug

The beaver trade was rough, the weather and the country harsh, and the mountain men who lived and worked there were rude and tough, many of them more savage than the Indians they found there. But buried deep within most men is a memory, however dim, of gentle things and stories learned at their mother's knee. Such a tale is this one. It's called The Jug.

The Jug

You ask me jist exac'ly how
  did I come by this liquor jug,
  how come I come to make it mine?
It's true, it's got a curious design
  — now that I will allow, like none I ever seen before —
  but how I made it my own property, well, fact is,
  I don't precisely know jist how.
As nigh as I can recomember,
  'twas in the skinny days o' late December,
  'long about the year o' twenty-five,
  when snow lay cold an' halfway deep
  enough to keep the Blackfoot liars
  fast beside their tipi fires,
  palaverin' about their coups an' sich
  — a time when beaver trappers thrive
  an' if a mountain man will match with work
  his greed for all the plunder he desires,
  a time to reap a harvest rich
  in close-haired beaver hides.
We'd been lucky, Patch Malone an' me,
  takin' our fair share o' beaver plews
  an' makin' all the meat two men could use,
  avoidin' ev'ry grizzly bear, stayin' loose from Bloods
  an' keepin' holt of our top hair,
  talkin' out the nights, so's to keep our reason,
  an' gen'rally a-biddin' fair to make o' this'n
  our most successful trappin' season.

O' course it wasn't altogether luck.
It takes a mite o' pluck to grit your teeth
  an' freeze your butt while searchin' underneath
  an icy pond to find a beaver in your trap,
  meanwhile a-wonderin' jist what
  might be awaitin' on the shore
  — a bear or perhaps a pair o' Kah-ee-nah young braves
  come out to even up a score.
But, all in all, the beaver trappin' hadn't been
  altogether bad that fall.
Howsomever, Patch an' me, we knew 'twas time to go
  an' find our winter lodgin' down amongst the Crow.
It's grief enough to spend your days a-dodgin'
  Big Bellies, Bloods, an' Pee-koo-nees,
  but I'd as lief fight all
  the Blackfoots in these Shinin' Hills
  as face the chills o' January snow.
We baled our plews an' struck our camp,
  saddled horses, packed our mules,
  an' headed mostly south an' somewhat west,
  satisfied we'd had the best
  o' trappin' 'fore the icy clamp o' winter in the Rockies
  replaced the chilly autumn damp.
We made fair time, ol' Patch an' me,
  breathin freer, yessiree! ever mile we put betwixt
  ourselves an' all those Blackfoot braves,
  who fixed to wear our hair or sell it to the Company.
As we drew nigh to Absaroka land
  I got to ruminatin' on a pert an' purty Absaroka lass
  belongin' to ol' High Owl's band
  an' wond'rin' if she'd be there waitin',
  greetin' me with open arms
  an' willin' still to trade her charms
  for beads an' cloth to stitch an' sich,

an' p'raps a lookin'-glass,
an' thinkin' shavin' ev'ry day
would be a measly price to pay
for all the pleasant nights we'd pass.

I reckon all my cogitatin', anticipatin' all the fun
  I figgered that there'd be there waitin',
    once we got to High Owl's band,
    stole my mind away from tendin' to the job I had at hand.
Next thing I know, an' quicker than it takes to tell,
  we come upon a big she-mother grizzly sow,
    a-trailin' both her cubs.
Oh, hotter than the hubs o' hell she was
  an' meaner than a bunch o' loco Blackfoot squaws.
Ol' Patch begun to shout
  an' all the mules they done a right-about
  an' scattered like a flock o' quail.
My horse he like to turned hisself
  completely inside out.
He swapped his ends so hellish quick
  the motion nearly made me sick
  an' then stampeded back along the trail,
  like all the imps an' fiends o' hell
  was hot upon his tail.
As like as not, he'd soon've run his fear away,
  but fate had somethin' more in store
  for this pore mountaineer that day.
I broke a rein a-tryin' jist to get him stopped.
He slipped an' fell. I rolled.
Then somethin' popped.
An' quicker than it can be told,
  I fetched up agin a tree, feelin' sicker than a pup,
  an' then I passed out cold.

When I awoke, sprawled out agin that tree,
  I knew instinctively my leg was broke.
All antigodlin bent it was, the foot was plumb askew,
  hot pokers throbbin' in my knee.
'Twas then I surely knew that life
  was purely done for me.
I huddled deep in my capote an' tried to bring to mind
  some things they wrote about my kind
  in Testament, but nothin' seemed to fit
  the trials of a man like me.
I wrenched around an' tried to sit,
  my back propped up agin the tree,
  picked up my Hawken rifle, checked the powder in the pan,
  then 'fore I knew what happened,
  I sort'a lost my memory.

Next thing I heard was little bells
  like Injuns wear for decoration.
Right then I swore that jist afore
  I departed God's creation an' went to my Eternity
  I'd take that sneakin' redskin 'long with me.
By then the winter moon had risen.
I cocked my rifle an' made sure
  I had dry powder 'neath the frizzen.
Then what I saw was purely queer.
Out there in the trees, I swear that I could see
  a bunch o' little deer an' comin' from amongst 'em
  a sight most truly weird —
  a portly little man all dressed in red,
  courtly in his walk an' German in his talk,
  his cheery face nigh disappeared
  behind a bushy silver beard.
He lifted up my head an' handed me this jug.
Then he begun to tug my busted leg.

I started off to beg him to belay
   — an' then I realized
   that all the pain had gone away.
" Drink up," sez he an' I drank deep
   o' liquor tastin' sweeter than the best of honey mead.
He smiled an' took a drink hisself
   an' winked his eye and in a little while
   I started in to yawn an' then I drifted off to sleep.

When I finally awoke, the little man was gone,
   but I had this jug an' my leg warn't broke.
An' there was Patch, a-shakin' me real hard.
"Wake up an' Happy Christmas, pard!" he sez
   an' cracks a smile as wide as Mississip —
   an' 'round about are all the mules an' packs
   an' even my loon horse,
   lookin' sorrowful an' leanin' on one hip.
We had a sip or two or so an' then 'twas surely time to go
   once more upon our journey to the Crow.
I tried to tell it all to Patch,
   but o' course he wouldn't listen.
I reckon that I dassn't fault him none,
   'cause who'd be likely to believe
   a history like this'n?

                  ॐ   ॐ   ॐ

Bullies

When most of us think of mountain men we envision big, tough, bearded, probably illiterate, irreverent rowdies wading freezing beaver ponds, fighting hostile Indians, confronting fierce grizzlies, and raising hell at a rollicking rendezvous. That is a fair picture of many of them, but it's not complete.

They weren't all big; Tom Fitzpatrick and Kit Carson certainly weren't. I'd say that all of them were tough, for if they weren't, they didn't survive. As for beards, those who had an eye for Indian maidens probably shaved rather than risk being called "Dog-face" by their intended light-o'-love. Regarding reverence, Jedediah Smith, for one, remained unquestionably pious throughout all his years in the mountains, which did not, however, prevent him from being a fearsome adversary in combat with hostile Indians.

Not being able to read, especially at that time, did not imply stupidity. Stupid men died early in the mountains. Some, such as Joe Meek, learned to read in winter camp, which they called Rocky Mountain College. Jim Bridger remained illiterate throughout his life. We'll likely never know, but it's worthwhile to wonder if he might have been dyslexic. Bridger had a keen mind, however, and a fantastic memory for topography, languages, Indian customs, business matters, and survival skills.

Some mountain men were thoughtful to a point of being philosophical, as we witness in James Clyman's journals. Beaver-trapping was often a solitary occupation and men had time to think about the world and their place in it.

Such a man tells some of his thoughts in the next story. It's called Bullies.

Bullies

Of all the hateful critters
  that surely irritate my pride
  it's gotta be a bully that I purely can't abide.
Out here in these mountains,
  follerin' the trapper's trade, a mountain man's alone a lot,
  which gives him ample time to think
  an' ponder how the world was made
  an' what is right an' what is not.
It ain't all dodgin' grizzly bear
  nor fightin' Injuns for your hair,
  nor goin' off to rendezvous for frolickin' an' drinkin'.
There's lots o' time for me an' you
  to do a heap o' thinkin'.
Now one thing I have figgered out,
  it's bullies what have brought about
  the sorry kind o' sitchy-ayshun
  that faces folks in ev'ry nation
  the length an' breadth o' God's Creation.

First of all, amongst a grand galore o' things,
  is jist how did we come, at first,
  to be so cursed with sich an awful thing as kings?
I reckon that I surely know
  jist how them critters got on top,
  without no one to make 'em stop,
  then made their evil power grow.
The whole thing started 'way back when

humans was jist barely men,
  callin' caves their home sweet home
an' livin' off the land,
  where'er their fancy let 'em roam.
Fact is, they warn't so different from our own trapper band.
An' then one day one feller
  who was bigger than the rest
  — an' meaner, too, I warrant you —
whupped all the other fellers an' declared
hisself the best-equipped to lead his little mob.
An' that is jist the way
  ol' Bully-King the First held sway an' got hisself the job.
'Course, all the littler bullies knew
  that they had oughter pay some heed,
so they come on a-swearin'
  they'll do their best to let him lead.
An' that is how it come to pass
  ol' Bully-King an' all his gang
got fat an' strong an' fearful rich,
  gettin' all the best o' meat an' sich,
while all the rest, for all them bullies cared,
could make their livin' eatin' grass.

Now it warn't too long afore
  another kind o' bully raised his wicked head.
This little feller warn't too strong,
  but he claimed that only he
knew good an' right from dreadful wrong
  — no one but he could talk with God
an' even with the dead.
Well, it didn't take ol' Bully-King
  much time to realize this little bully feller
is gainin' power far beyond his puny mortal size
by scarin' ever'body with his curses an' his prayers

an' buildin' wealth by makin' his what formerly was theirs.
But 'stead o' clubbin' him to death
  or stompin' him beneath his heel,
  ol' Bully-King gets crafty-cute
  an' offers him a partnership
  — what you might call a deal.
Brute strength an' superstition
  make a fearsome combination,
  tellin' us jist who will take an' who will do the givin',
  an' how an' when to do it if we want to keep on livin'.

My father an' my gran'dad sent
  King Georgie's troops a-packin',
  but after all the Redcoats went,
  tyrants o' the home-grown kind
  most sartinly warn't lackin'.
Instead o' struttin' peacocks called the agents o' the Crown,
  we spawned a generation o' bullies of our own
  to keep the common people down.
There's pettifoggin' lawyers an'
  slave-ownin' pluto-ristocrats,
  treatin' workin' folks jist like a bunch o' common rats,
  an' politicians makin' law
  like spiders spinnin' webs for flies,
  cuttin' common people down to puny size.
An' there's hardly no escapin' tax-collectors scrapin' 'til
  you're absolutely raw, backed up by the sheriff an'
  his bullies o' the Law.

That's precisely what was stickin' in my craw!
It's the worst o' sitchy-ayshuns a body ever saw!
So I up an' left the settlements
  — best decision that I ever made —
  an' come out to these mountains

for practicin' the trapper's trade.
Us free trappers take our chances an' do the best we can
  and there ain't a man amongst us who'd bow to any man.

But bein' in the mountains ain't always what you'd think.
We still get braggin' bullies like
  the late an' unlamented would-be mountain man Mike Fink.
Mike Fink was a riverman, keelboats were his game,
  an' 'twas on the Mississippi he gained his ugly fame.
He was a brawlin' bully an' a deadly marksman, too
  — his heart as black as Egypt's night,
  cruel an' murd'rous in a fight,
  he'd kick an' butt an' gouge an' bite
  - a devil through an' through.
An' then in eighteen-twenty-two
  Fink signed with Gen'ral Ashley's crew
  to go a-trappin' beaver plew upon the High Missourah,
  bringin' his two pards along.
Carpenter an' Talbot was their names
  an' jist as fond as Fink o' deadly games,
  neither of 'em knowin' right from wrong.
Now Carpenter an' Fink they had a sport
  that's sure to make your life too short.
They'd shoot a cup o' whiskey from off each other's head
  at fifty-sixty yards, reasonin' since they was pards,
  neither one'd end up dead.
But up at winter camp upon the Musselshell,
  Carpenter an' Fink they had a fallin'-out
  about a purty Injun squaw.
They both was feelin' mighty raw,
  but Fink he says it makes no nevermind,
  let's find a way the better man can win
  an' play our little game agin.
Well, truth to tell, Fink's copper coin was tossed

an', sure as hell, 'twas Carpenter who lost.
Carpenter he reckons how Mike Fink has got it planned,
  but bully though he is, he's got a lot o' sand.
He hands his guns an' possibles to Talbot standin' by,
  then hikes out sixty paces, turns an' spits,
  an' stares his rival in the eye,
  then puts the whiskey cup upon his head.
Mike Fink he aims an' fires
  an' like ev'rybody reckoned, ol' Carpenter is dead.
'Course, Fink he claims his aim was true,
  but all of us most surely knew
  he'd squared accounts with Carpenter
  'thout reckonin' with Talbot, who wasn't nearly through.
Well, Fink, the braggin' bully,
  got drunk an' had to tell, so Talbot pulls his pistol
  an' sends Fink off to hell.
No one thought to punish Talbot,
  for we was way beyond the Law,
  an' Talbot he was grizzly-mean,
  the worst o' men you ever saw.
No proper trapper had been hurt
  an' Fink had got his just de-sert.
But ev'ry bully needs to boast
  an' it warn't so long, two-three months at most,
  'fore Talbot goes an' drowns hisself,
  swimmin' Teton River, runnin' high in spring.
'Twas sure a time to dance an' sing,
  a thing for us to shout about.
All o' them three bullies had cancelled one another out.

Still an' all, I've found it's best
  a man should stand his ground an' fight
  for what he thinks is proper, legitimate, an' right.
Which 'minds me of a bully at rendezvous in thirty-five,

a vicious, giant French Canuck,
an' how 'twas only his good luck
that let 'im leave that place alive.
We was campin' on the Seeds-kee-dee,
  awaitin' Fitz an' his supplies,
  when Andy Drips shows up in camp
  an' brings along this Frenchy scamp.
Shunar was his name, but he calls hisself the Mountain King
  an' sev'ral other fancy lies.
Well, he beat the livin' hell
  out o' most of all the Frenchy crew
  an' then declares he's tougher than any white American
  he's like to meet at this here rendezvous.
'Bout then he puts his dirty paws
  on sev'ral friendly Injun squaws.
They got scared an' started in to cry
  — an' 'mongst 'em was a maiden
  who'd caught Kit Carson's eye,
  a little half-pint feller who worked for Billy Bent,
  so short by time you'd see him he had already went.
Young Kit had not a jot o' swagger
  an' sartinly he warn't no bragger,
  so when he stared the big Canuck squarely in the eye,
  we knew that one or both o' them
  was surely bound to die.
"You keep your hands off o' my squaw
  an' shut your braggin' Frenchy maw,
  without no ifs nor ands nor buts,
  or else I'll rip your stinkin' guts!"
Shunar glares an' then he seen in Carson's eyes the look
  o' somethin' like a wolverine,
  what Frenchies call a carcajou, an animal what ain't so big
  but what'll chaw your leg in two.
Shunar backs off an' runs to fetch his rifle an' his horse

an' then comes roarin' back to camp,
declarin' that he'll ketch young Kit
an' swearin' that Kit's sure to die.
Kit don't waste no time, o' course.
  He loads an' primes his pistol
  an' grabs his Injun horse,
  then rides to meet the Frenchman, pure murder in his eye.
What happened after that occurred
  quicker than it takes to tell.
The rifle an' the pistol barked an' then the Frenchman fell.
The bully's ball had clipped Kit's hair,
  the powder burned his eye.
The Frenchman he lay sprawlin' there
  an' Carson swore the Frog'd die.
A score or more o' pistols was offered to young Kit,
  then Carson saw the kind o' job his pistol ball had done
  an' reckoned he'd already had the very best of it.
That Frenchman, in the future, wouldn't bully anyone.
  Kit's pistol ball had smashed his fist
  an' plumb tore up the bully's wrist
  an' shattered all the forearm bone
  'bout from the elbow down.
So from here there's naught to fear.
Shunar's best career is bound
  to be some sort o' circus clown.

If you're lookin' for philosophy in this here tale o' mine,
  it's up here in these mountains
  a bully jist don't shine.
They're better off in settlements,
  under cover o' the Law.
Out here they get comeuppance,
  the rule o' fang an' claw.
I'd jist as liefer hang 'em,

but speakin' plain, as like as not,
the most of us'll likely take a careful aim
an' send 'em off to hell with a final partin' shot.

           ∾   ∾   ∾

Two-toes Le Beau

The hardships and perils of beaver-trappers living in the harsh wilderness of the early Nineteenth Century Rocky Mountains were many and great. Survival required skill, courage, and fortitude, and, preferably, a fair amount of luck. The dubious hero of this tale, a French-Canadian trapper named Jean LeBeau, possessed the first three in considerable abundance, but good fortune eluded him, at least on one particular day.

Two-toes Le Beau

Y'see that trapper mincin' 'long,
  trav'lin' more'n somewhat dainty?
He's steppin' kinda lightly, don'tcha know?
Sorta goin' tippy-toe, now ain't he?
He's a trapper we all know,
  a French-Canuck, who, one cold an' wintry day,
  kinda run plumb short o' luck.
His mama named him Jean LeBeau,
  but, if ye like, I'll tell ye how
  he's knowed as Frenchy Two-toes now.
LeBeau he be a righteous mountaineer
  an' nearly always brings to camp
  his own fair share o' plew.
And in a fight he stands his ground
  as good as any French-Canuck that I have ever found.
But Jean he had one troublin' flaw.
  He loved to lie abed long past the time the rest of us
  had risen, answered Nature's call,
  fed the critters, broke our fast,
  an' readied fer another day
  o' hikin' 'long the cricks an' streams
  where beavers like to stay.
No matter thunderbolts be flyin'
  or even if the rain be pourin',
  ol' Jean be lyin' fast asleep, competin' with his snorin'.
So one day it comes about that Jean rolls out
  his robes when nearly ever'body's gone.
He rubs his eyes an' greets the day

with belches and, o' course, a yawn.
Feelin' more'n somewhat groggy,
  he's yankin' on his soggy moccasins as quick he could,
  when he finds he's got not a single stick o' firewood
  to brew his mornin' tea.
He grabs an axe an' then attacks
  a nearby holler tree.
But sleepy as our Frenchy be, after jist a couple whacks,
  the axe it slips from out his grip, an' slices off a toe.
"Sacré merde!" he yells, which tells
  the rest of us that Frenchy's gone
  an' bought hisself a sure-'nough heap o' woe.
LeBeau, for all his faults an' bluff,
  be one tough mountain man.
So quicker than we think he can,
  that iron-hearted Frenchy scamp
  picks hisself from off the ground,
  grabs his gun an' possibles, an' tramps on out o' camp.
He reckons losin' jist one toe don't make no nevermind,
  so off he goes, inspectin' traps,
  like all his beaver-huntin' kind.

Jean comes onto his beaver pond
  an' spies his float-stick ridin' free,
  which tells 'im he has gained a plew.
Right off, he jumps into the water,
  like any self-respectin' trappin' man
  had always better oughter do.
He wades out to his floatin' stick
  an' grabs the chain to haul the beaver out.
Problem is, the critter ain't completely dead.
  He ain't about to quit.
Instead, he bit another toe clean off.
Ol' Jean lets out a shout an' coughs an' spits

an' splits that beaver's skull in two,
  but there warn't a single useful thing
  that Jean LeBeau could do.
The harm was done.
The daily count o' toes he'd lost
  now wasn't only one, but two.
Cussin' more'n somewhat, the big Canuck goes sloshin'
  through the muck to shore, plannin' to restore his luck
  by trappin' still one beaver more
  — an' mebbe sev'ral more beyond —
  from out that cussèd beaver pond.
But whilst he's occupied in cockin' his rusty beaver trap,
  his muddy, bloody moccasin slides off the slipp'ry spring
  an' Snap!
He's lost another toe.
LeBeau he calls on all his saints on earth,
  in hell, an' even some in heaven.
The total sum o' toes he'd kept
  amounted to no more'n seven.

Whilst Frenchy is plumb busy with
  his self-commiseratin', he hears a most tremenjous roar
  that sets the trees reverberatin'.
He whirls an' sees a huge ol' grizzly boar
  'twixt hisself an' his rifle gun.
He knows it ain't no good to run,
  so Jean he shinnies up the closest tree,
  a skinny little aspen, measly as can be.
As Frenchy is a-climbin' up,
  he's trav'lin' jist a mite too slow.
The bear he nearly catches up an' snatches off another toe.

LeBeau gits perched amongst the topmost limbs.
He's singin' half-forgotten holy hymns

mixed in with desp'rate prayin'.
Ol' Griz, 'cause he ain't equipped to climb,
  commenced to set the tree a-swayin',
  pushin' back an' forth fer all his mighty worth,
  whilst Jean be swingin' forth an' back,
  fearin' that the tree'll crack
  an' he'll come tumbling down to earth.
Then jist when Ephraim gits LeBeau nigh onto the ground,
  he slips his grip an' sees the tree suddenly rebound,
  then re-commences roarin', sizzlin' hot,
  when he sees the sad result.
The tree springs up an' sends LeBeau
  a-soarin', like as if he's shot plumb off a catapult.

When Frenchy quits his aviatin' through the air,
  he 'lights way high upon the river bank.
But afore he gits a chance to thank
  his lucky stars, he spies a big ol' mama painter cat
  emergin' from her lair.
Now Jean don't need no urgin'. Quick as scat,
  he scuttles back'ards down her hidey-hole,
  content to keep together, least fer now,
  his body an' his soul.
.Natcherly the Mama Cat ain't takin' kindly to
  this smelly interloper in her den.
She snarls an' growls an' then she howls,
  snappin' with her deadly fangs
  an' swipin' with her claws so fast
  she's surely breakin' Nature's Laws, I promise you —
  well, possibly, as like as not.
An' all that Jean LeBeau has got
  is jist his puny skinnin' knife
  fer the sheer presarvin' of his simple, sinful life.
He's jabbin' an' a-stabbin'

to keep the painter cat at bay,
when suddenly he feels the grab
o' one hellacious, awful pain,
which, in other circumstances,
would'a sent him on his way with absolutely no delay.
But now he's trapped, enwrapt in rock,
imprisoned, with the fearsome shock
o' somethin' nasty nibblin' on
all that he's got left o' toes.
'Bout then the dismal thought arose
that what was chewin' on his toes
— enough to make a good man bitter —
was Mama Painter's hungry litter.
LeBeau was in a righteous tight,
lackin' proper means to fight,
with Mama Painter at his head, devoutly dedicated to
ol' Jean's complete defeat,
an' even less agin the cubs a-gnawin' at his feet.
Jist when LeBeau is losin' heart
an' mostly all his hope, he chanced to spy ol' Ephraim
come a-shamblin' up the slope.
The painter cat she sees him, too,
an' hesitates a moment, not knowin' what to do.
LeBeau's a bloody nuisance, refusin', like he is, to go —
but a grizzly bear is, after all,
her ancestral nat'ral foe.
Instinct wins out, an' so without no further hesitation,
the painter cat, she turns about an' heads on out,
intent on confrontation.

Frenchy wastes no time, a-tall,
in wrigglin' out his sepulcher.
'Twas time that he bestir hisself
an' head fer gentler neighborhoods

an' company he'd much prefer
to the howlin', growlin', yowlin' pair
engaged in deadly war jist down the hillside there.
LeBeau he saw no need to hide,
  fer Ephraim an' the Mama Cat
was much too occupied, jist then,
to pay much heed or give a damn
  'bout measly mortal mountain men.

Ol' Jean he wends his limpin' way
  somehow on back to camp, gimpin' 'long an' listin',
  sometimes left an' sometimes right,
  sorta like a ship adrift on some wild an' stormy ocean
  — an altogether sorry case o' faulty locomotion.
When Jean comes hobblin' into camp, we saw
  his moccasins was in a state o' dreadful need o' cobblin'.
Shredded nearly to the knee,
  they made it plain fer all to see
  LeBeau's remainin' toes were few.
Accidents and depredation had whittled down his count o' toes
  to purely nothin' more than two.

Natcherly we gathered 'round
  an' laid the hurtin' Frenchy down
  an' did whatever good we could with poultices of herbs,
  together with what else we found.
An' then, Alas! we dug out all the booze we had.
Ol' Jean drank deep an' fast, until, at last,
  our friend confessed
  his vast accumulation of that restorative libation
  by then had got 'im feelin' not so bad.
We reckoned, then, he was presarved enough to keep
  an' so we let 'im fall asleep.

Next mornin' Jean LeBeau be much improved.
An' though he hasn't moved from out his robes,
  he's vergin' on pure merriment
  an' even takin' nourishment.
He puts aside the moccasin
  he's trimmin' down to make it smaller
  an' drains a final swaller from out his cow-horn cup
  an' says to all of us,
  "Mes amis, m'friends, ye know I ain't inclined to bawl,
  but,'pears to me, some days, I find,
  it jist ain't hardly worth
  all the consarned fuss an' pother
  to bother gittin' up a-tall!"

ও   ও   ও

Tracks

Mountain men learned their trade on the job. Some had a head start
on their comrades, especially if they had learned to shoot and had
acquired some elementary woodcraft in the forests around their
eastern farm communities. But all that was merely kindergarten when
they arrived in the Rocky Mountains and confronted the problems and
perils posed by hostile Indians, wild beasts, and the weather. There
they soon learned the myriad skills of the experienced fur trappers;
and if they weren't apt pupils, they perished.

Tracks

Afore you greedy-gutted greenhorns
  — an' sich is what you sartinly appear to be —
  can start to balin' up a stock o' beaver plews
  an' gain the riches that've set
  your puny pilgrim brains to burnin',
  it's plain for sich as me to see
  ye need to do an' awful heap o' learnin'.
You stand in dreadful need
  o' sartin kinds o' special knowledge.
Your schoolin's jist begun
  in this here Rocky Mountain College.
You need to read the seasons by the sun
  an' learn to load an' shoot dead plumb
  a pistol an' your rifle gun an' run a stock o' rifle balls
  an' all the calls o' birds an' mountain critters,
  an' how to judge your companyeros
  — who's got sand an' which amongst 'em are jist quitters.
You got to know jist where an' how to set your winter camp
  an' how to dry your powder when it's damp.
There's purely a galore o' stuff
  o' which you'll need to get the knack,
  but mebbe toughest of 'em all
  is learnin' how to read a track.
Why, I'd as liefer turn stone blind
  than lose my sense o' beaver sign.
An' trackin' game'll learn you that
  not hardly any two are quite the same.
You'll want to know the deer you're stalkin',

whether it be buck or doe, an' if it's lean or rollin' fat
  — or if you're trailin' wapiti, whether it's a bull or cow,
  an' jist how fast the critter's walkin'.
You need to read the tracks o' riders passin' through
  an' how to cover up your own
  — an' once the basic facts are known,
  no one'll be surprisin' you.
You'll need to hide your peltry caches
  an' learn to read the ashes of an Injun horse-thief's fire,
  knowin' when he left an' pushin' jist how many horses,
  whether they be fresh or if they have begun to tire
  — an' jist how many horse-thieves
  an' how fast they're trav'lin'.
Tracks'll help you in unrav'lin' mysteries
  afore they turn to miseries.
The way each tribe an' band'll shape their moccasins'll tell
  if it's pesky Blackfoots or friendly Snakes out there.
The difference it makes might let you pilgrims keep your hair.
Injuns take to readin' sign like parsons read a book.
  You can learn it, too, jist fine.
  It's knowin' how an' where to look.

Which 'minds me now of ol' Sluefoot Magee
  an' a queersome kind o' history.
It started sev'ral winters back
  when early snows'd caught us up around the Yellerstone.
Experience'd taught us well, so we set up a winter camp,
  postponin' beaver-trappin' 'til the spring,
  diggin' in agin the cold an' damp
  an' glad there's plenty of us,
  for hivernatin' ain't much fun when you're doin' it alone.
Meat was plenty thereabouts an' firewood galore.
A mountain man'd hardly wish for more.

There was nigh a score o' men
  — Joe Meek an' Doc an' Frapp an' Bill,
  an' Jim an' Tinker Ben, a half-a-dozen Englishmen,
  some Delawares, an' me, besides a little Irishman.
His name was Pat Magee.
Magee went trampin' out o' camp
  one cold an' snowy afternoon
  an' reckoned that he'd bag a wapiti
  an' we'd be eatin' meat real soon.
Magee he found some sign an' he commenced to foller,
  thinkin' on the taste o' wapiti.
Then jist as he was nearin' the border of a clearin',
  ol' Pat let out a holler.
A big ol' grizzly boar was roarin',
  plumb hot as hell beneath his collar,
  makin' straight for Pat Magee.
'Fore you could blink an eye to see,
  ol' Pat Magee he climbed a tree.
He knew he was too close to run.
This way he kept his rifle gun.
Paddy climbed as high as possibly he could,
  whilst down below Ol' Ephraim
  was gruntin' and a-slobberin' and a-clawin' bark an' wood.
He set that tree to shakin'
  so bad it kept Magee from takin' aim.
Then branches broke beneath him an' down ol' Paddy came.
The grizzly bear was waitin'.
'Twarn't no time for hesitatin.
Magee he aimed his gun an' sent the critter off to hell.
Ol' Ephraim spun around an' fell a-sprawlin' on his back.
Last thing that Pat Magee recalled
  was hearin' both his leg bones crack.

We found ol' Pat Magee out there,

pinned plumb beneath that grizzly bear.
Joe Meek was first to speak, but when he spoke,
  nobody learned a thing. He said,
  "I reckon both his legs are broke."
We packed Magee on back to camp
  an' tried to ease his pain an' cramp,
  but it was ever'body's bettin'
  them legs o' his plumb needed settin'.
Both his legs was badly busted,
  but not a one amongst us trusted what we knew
  'bout settin' broken bones
  — but each of us most surely knew
  that from out this trappin' crew
  some new-elected surgeon had to do.
Natcherly nobody volunteered.
Ev'ry man amongst us was afeared
  to try his hand an' seek to mend
  the fractures of our Irish friend.
Then ol' Bill Williams jumped onto his feet
  and in that cracked an' shrilly voice o' his
  ol' Solitaire begun to bleat,
  "I found the key for ol' Magee that's sure to turn the lock!
We got a man amongst us that we been callin' Doc!"
Doc Newell he commenced to yell, tellin' us to go to hell,
  an' said that "Doc" was jist his handle
  an' that he couldn't hold a candle to
  a cross-eyed baby nurse —
  an' if he should attend Magee,
  the sorry Irisher would certainly be worse.
His protests made no nevermind.
Us trappers we were glad to find a goat to do a dirty job
  an' fob responsibility on any someone else,
  no matter how he whined.
Magee was suff'rin' somethin' dreadful from the shock

an' runnin' him close second was
  our unexperienced surgeon Doc.
Joe Meek took pity on 'em both an' dug
  amongst his possibles, then offered them his jug.
Doc knew it wouldn't do to shirk,
  so "Doctor Newell" set to work.
Well, first he'd yank an' then he'd tug
  an' pause to take another slug
  from out o' Joe Meek's whiskey jug.
Ere long ol' Doc was purely sweatin',
  gettin' drunker by the minute.
There surely warn't no logic in it,
  an' Newell he was purely shook,
  still bound to do whate'er it took
  in patchin' up ol' Pat Magee,
  though Doc knew less than bugger-all
  about the art o' surgery.
Doc grabbed a tithe o' willer withes
  an' fashioned up some wooden splints.
An' since there warn't no bandages,
  some buckskin leggin's made some lace.
Doc tidied up them willer splints
  an' tied 'em up real tight.
Then Newell, well, he passed right out.
He didn't even say goodnight.

Next day, we gathered 'round Magee,
  early, jist as day was bornin',
  sober as a box o' Mormons
  on a sacred Sabbath mornin'.
One look was all it took to tell
  our friend Magee was in for hell!
Though Doc had done his sorry best,
  one foot was on its way back east,

the other purely pointed west!
No trapper in that camp would try to put to rights what Doc
  — an' Joe Meeks's jug — had set awry.
From that day on, all thanks to Doc,
  Pat's tracks'd look like six o'clock.
An' that is how it come to be we call him ol' Sluefoot Magee.

Magee was tough as ary Mick as ever left the Sod,
  an' soon as he could leave his bed,
  he learned hisself to crawl
  an' then to haul hisself ahead an' finally to plod,
  but you could always tell Pat's tracks
  by the antigodlin way he trod.
Come spring Magee was fit as e'er he'd be,
  with beaver season standin' nigh.
He bade our sorry bunch goodbye
  an' went off trappin' on his own.
He reckoned he could learn to do his trappin' work alone
  an' if he couldn't do it, why then, o' course, he'd die.

One damp an' snowy mornin', ol' Sluefoot he set out from camp
  to work his line o' beaver traps.
He checked his powder, ball, an' caps,
  for he'd spied Blackfoot sign about his lonely neighborhood
  — an' Blackfoots of whatever kind
  don't promise any white-eyes good.
Pat rode his pony 'bout a mile on down the crick,
  but after 'while the brush become
  more'n jist a trifle thick.
He tethered up his horse onto a willer root,
  then slung his rifle gun an' went ahead afoot.
After payin' visits to all his beaver sets,
  ol' Sluefoot gets to circlin' 'round
  his beaver-trappin' ground,

then doublin' back on his old track
a couple hunnerd yards below the place his horse is tied,
nibblin' on the cottonwoods an' pawin' in the snow.
He clamped his saddle on real tight
  an' tied his beaver plews behind
  an' then commenced to find his way on back to camp
to eat an' sleep the night.

'Bout then, a bunch o' Blackfoots come
  a-trailin' through an' find
  the prints o' Sluefoot's moccasins.
Then from the ashes of his pipe they know
  that Sluefoot's of the white-eyes kind,
  since Injuns never smoke along the trail.
Before they smoke, they're hunkered down
  all peaceful, a-squattin' on their tail.
Now Blackfoots think no more o' killin' whites
  than swattin' at a fly,
  an' 'sides, ol' Pat was trespassin'
  an' stealin' Blackfoot trappin' rights.
This partic'lar Blackfoot bunch
  was headed by an ol' Siksika chief
  by name o' Barkin' Spider an' by his heathen Injun lights
  this unknown white intruder warn't
  no better than a common thief
  an' that 'twas only right an' fair
  that these Siksikas take his hair.
But jist afore ol' Barkin' Spider tells his men to go,
  he studies Sluefoot's tracks again
  an' sez, "It's plain as travois drags in snow,
  these are the tracks of two one-legged men!
  One travels to the east, the other's goin' west.
  It's best we split our band in two, and then
  we'll each count coup upon a different one-legged man."

No matter howsomever much they'd look,
  they found no track or trace
  o' peg or wooden leg or crutch,
  nor stick nor staff nor shepherd's crook.
The tracks kept goin', never stoppin'.
They reckoned that he must be hoppin'.
Them Injuns they plumb drawed a blank
  where Pat jumped off a ten-foot bank.
They sort'a thought they understood
  jist how a man with one leg could
  jump down from off that ten-foot drop
  — but jist how could that other man
  get up that bank with jist a single hop?
When they come to where Magee had doubled back,
  Bad Wind, Barkin' Spider's son,
  saw where Sluefoot's tracks had run together,
  a couple hunnerd paces down below the place
  where Pat had left his pony on a tether.
So Bad Wind thinks he understands
  an' opens up his mouth:
  "The tracks show two two-legged men,
  one walkin' north, the other on his way down south.
  Jist maybe those one-legged men
  have found their missin' legs again!"
But Barkin' Spider has his say:
  "My son has eyes jist like a bat in light o' day!
  The count of tracks is four — two left feet, two right.
  Look again, my son with eyes of bat!
  These are the tracks of four one-legged men.
  I'll bet my feathered lance on that!"
The mood amongst them Injuns was anythin' but merry.
Nobody said it right out loud,
  but all o' this was lookin' scary.

But curiosity's what killed the cat, they say,
  so they went trailin' on a way, until they come onto
  where Sluefoot mounts his horse.
O' course by now they figgered they
  was in the land o' single-legged men,
  so they reckoned two o' them had climbed aboard the horse,
  while the other two had gone into the willers once again.
They follered back along o' Sluefoot's pony track
  an' trailed him into camp,
  where Pat was snorin' fast asleep, his feet agin the fire
  to keep away the cold an' damp.
So when them Blackfoots come a-sneakin' 'round,
  they see ol' Sluefoot sleepin' sound,
  all calm an' peaceful on the snowy ground.
They reckon they'll jist kill him quick
  an' tie his hair upon a wipin'-stick,
  then set about the swipin' of all his stock an' plunder
— which'd be their just reward
for puttin' any white-eyes under.
Then what they saw most surely made
  each superstitious heathen clap
  his hand to cover up his mouth,
  'cause what they saw was Sluefoot's feet
  — one goin' north, the other surely headin' south.

Now Injun's ain't accustomed to the sight o' cripples 'mongst
  wild critters or in humankind.
You won't hardly never find that sich a critter can survive.
It's rare to see a growed-up cripple still alive.
So when ol' Barkin' Spider saw ol' Sluefoot's crippled feet,
  the old chief's fear an' wonderment was purty near complete.
His teachin's told him that Magee'd been surely touched,
  protected by the Everlastin' Spirit's hand,
  an' harmin' such a critter could

mebbe bring bad medicine an' such
  upon the whole Siksika band.
Young Bad Wind an' another half-growed buck
  was less inclined to grant ol' Pat Magee such luck.
They opined that since they found him there
  they'd kill him now an' take his hair.
But Barkin' Spider says he can't allow
  the harmin' o' this crippled Mick
  — jist like an Injun is forbid to harm a ravin' lunatic.
An' 'sides, the white-eyes' tracks've tricked
  the hawk-eyed Blackfoots all day long.
So now they'd best be mountin' up an' movin' right along.

When Pat wakes up, he sees the tracks
  o' moccasins an' ponies there
  but never guesses jist how close
  he comes to partin' with his hair.
So Pat goes on and lives his life,
  whistlin' some old Irish tune,
  trappin' when he wanted to
  an' makin' tracks that looked a lot
  jist like half-after-noon.

I know this tale is gospel true
  that I have jist been tellin' you,
  'cause Barkin' Spider said 'twas so,
  one freezin' winter night when we
  — that is, m'self an' ol' Sluefoot Magee —
  was hunkered by a tipi fire's warmin' glow,
  a-list'nin' to the ol' chief tellin' us
  the facts o' this here queersome history
  an' realizin' if it warn't for Sluefoot's antigodlin feet,
  his topknot surely would be danglin'
  from a pole in this same lodge,

all stretched an' dried an' braided neat.

Magee can come an' go with them the balance of his days.
He's knowed amongst the Blackfoots as
 the Man-who-walks-both-ways.

Carcane

The longer the beaver-trapping fraternity remained in the mountains the more elaborate their tall tales became. In time, however, yarns concerning hairbreadth escapes from hostile Indians and ferocious grizzly bears inevitably palled and it became necessary to reach out to the realm of mythical creatures and situations to provide grist for the story-telling mill. An excellent source of raw material lay in the superstitions of the highly-suggestible French-Canadian trappers and engagés. Among their many inventions was an elusive beast they called the Carcagne. American mountain men naturally modified the name to "Carcane" and that is how it is pronounced in the following tale, Carcane.

Carcane

You pilgrims who jist recently
  have come out to these mountains
  have surely heard a heap o' trash
  concernin' mountains made o' glass
  an' ever-boilin' fountains,
  an' other forms o' God's an' Nature's prodigies.
Well, I assure you that all these things an' more
  are truly what you greenhorns have in store.
But what I aim to tell about
  concerns a mountain animal
  that I can surely do without.

There's them that's seen the elephant
  — at least that's what they say —
  standin' out an' grazin', plain as day.
Big ol' hairy critters, a tail at either end,
  an' teeth like iv'ry swords.
Jist one o' them could send
  a regiment o' mountain men
  on down the trail to Kingdom Come.
An' not a body knows jist where
  they might be comin' from.
  There's other fearsome critters
  that men've said you'll find up there,
  like cross-bred wolverines
  that are the size o' grizzly bear,
  and elk with antlers big as crystal chandeliers,
  too big to shoot with jist a rifle gun,

what have no trouble mowin' down
  a mile o' standin' trees when they commence to run,
  whilst buglin' fit to bust your ears.
Well, I don't know an' have no way
  o' testin' out the truth o' what ol' Gabe
  an' sev'ral of the others say,
  but what I aim to tell to you this day
  is history as true an' right as rain,
  at least, concernin' a big mountain beast
  the Nor'west Frenchies call Carcane.
We was trappin' up near Beaverhead,
  north an' west o' country known
  by trappers as the Yellerstone.
The streams was rich, like Bridger said,
  in first-rate beaver plews,
  'bout all a mountain man could use.
. The daily yield was five or six a man!
Meantime we kept our eyeballs peeled
  to scan for Injun sign
  'cause we was on the Blackfoots' land
  an' Blackfoots dearly love to find
  a beaver-poachin' mountain man.
'Twas late one autumn afternoon
  an' I was trampin' back to camp,
  hummin' up a happy tune,
  six beaver plews upon my shoulder,
  when, comin' 'round a giant boulder,
  I saw a sight that nearly made me swoon.
Standin' in a clearin' there
  was what at first I took to be a grizzly bear.
But lookin' close, I rubbed my eyes
  as I begun to realize
  this critter was near twice the size
  of any bear that I had ever seen.

An' then he turned his shaggy head.
  Right then I guessed I'd soon be dead.
I'm sure I turned a bilious shade o' green.
The head that should'a been a grizzly bear,
  I truly swear, it wasn't there.
  It was a hungry timber wolf instead!
An' lashin' out behind him on the trail
  was a painter's long an' slinky tail!
The blood it drained from out my brain.
I reckoned that I'd gone insane.
What I was facin' up to there
  warn't no common grizzly bear.
    'Twas what the Frenchies call Carcane!

Now, one thing 'bout a French Canuck,
  he's long on song, but short on pluck,
  which means he's apt to light a shuck
  an' hardly never trust to luck
  an' plant his feet an' stand an' fight.
But later, when he has no fright,
  he'll likely tell o' ghosts an' hants
  that come upon him in the night,
  all for the sake o' justifyin'.
  I call it naught but downright lyin'!
So when I'd hear the Frenchies tell
  o' critters come straight out o' hell,
  I reckoned it was jist their way
  o' savin' face an' facin' yet another day
  — an' for the likes o' them 'twas jist as well.
But now I knew that some, at least,
  o' what the Frenchies said was true.
What stood before me was a beast
  composed o' flesh an' blood an' bone
  an' shaggy hair an' teeth an' claws,

despite a combination that defied
the most o' God's creation laws.
Right then he spied me hangin' 'round
an' he let out a dreadful sound,
a blendin' of a snarl an' growl
an' endin' in a fearsome howl.
He lifted straight upon his hocks an' sniffed.
I guessed unless I got the gift o' wings, at least,
that beast was sartin sure to give
this sinful mountain man short shrift.
I swung my rifle up an' tried to take a bead,
but then my hands was shakin' so, indeed,
that when I shot, the ball went wide
an' only creased his hairy hide.
He howled an' snarled an' growled
an' then commenced to beller.
My belly turned a half a dozen shades o' yeller
an' I was purely makin' tracks on down the mountainside.
There surely warn't no place to hide
an' climbin' trees would do no good.
The wildcat side o' Carcane could
most prob'ly shinny up a tree
a damnsight quicker, far, than me.
O' course I dropped my plews an' gun
when I begun to run this race
in which I'd better be the winner,
or else I'd be the Carcane's dinner.
Sartin death was second place.
I felt his stinkin' breath a-blowin' on my face
as he begun to overtake my ever-slowin' pace
an' heard him yippin' and a-caterwaulin',
his claws a-rippin' up the ground,
bawlin' like a babe an' snufflin' like a hog.
An' then I spied a holler log.

I dived an' wriggled up inside,
  surprised that I was still alive.
That beast was fitten to be tied,
  mad as hell that I'd deprived him of
  at least a tough an' scrawny feast.
He screamed an' clawed an' chawed on bark an' wood,
  but when it seemed 'twould do no good,
  he tried another ploy.
He hugged an' tugged that holler log
  as if it was a baby's toy
  an' ripped it clean from out the ground,
  then twirled it twice around his head
  an' threw it down the hill.
I reckon I'd be rollin' still,
  except the log fetched up, instead, agin a rock.
  I'd hafta say 'twas quite a thrill.
I was a sight relieved, an' that's a fact,
  to find my wooden armor still pretty much intact.
The Carcane was plumb disappointed.
His dinner plans was all disjointed.
An' I could hear his teeth a-gnashin'
  whilst he was occupied in trashin' up the landscape
  in a plumb pluperfect dreadful fashion.
At last he got hisself plumb tuckered out
  an' sat hisself upon the log to rest
  an' mebbe puzzle out the best o' ways
  to get me snookered out o' my safe hidin' place.
He was sittin' right above my face
  an' next to him I saw a hole
  where once a limb had grown.
An' now an' then I'd see his tail a-lashin' side to side,
  whilst Carcane sat upon his throne, calca'latin' homicide.
Quick as thought I reached an' got
  my fingers on his tail an' yanked

it down inside, then tied it in a lover's-knot,
  an' added one half-hitch besides.
At first he screamed an' then he cried
  an' then he loosed a fearsome roar
  that shook the very forest floor.
I scurried from my hidin' place,
  but all too quickly learned that I
  had only got myself involved in yet another race.
'Twas true the burden that he bore
  made Carcane slower than before.
But though he dragged that holler tree,
  he was a shade more quick than me.
I could feel his rancid breath,
  smellin' like eternal death,
  peelin' hide right off my back.
The farther that he dragged that tree
  the more he seemed to get the knack.
With space between us gettin' shorter
  I knew that I had better orter conjure up a better plan
  before Carcane reduced the span.
I ran between a pair o' trees
  a-growin' 'bout two yards apart.
'Twas then I had a happy thought
  that positively warmed my heart.
I stopped an' whirled an' stood with both my arms akimbo
  an' hoped this warn't my ticket to
  sweet Heaven, Hell, or Limbo.
Ol' Carcane he plumb took the bait
  an' charged me like a buffler herd,
  as if he couldn't wait to sate
  his hunger an' his dreadful hate.
He run between that pair o' trees
  an' then that beast appeared to freeze.
The log hung up an' checked his run

— an' that is where the fun begun!
His titanic weight an' forward speed
  operated to exceed the strength o' Carcane's shaggy hide.
It peeled his pelt back from his nose,
  removin' all the bones inside.
  Carcane committed suicide!
  A fitting end, I do propose.
An' whilst I was a-standin' there,
  six hunnerd pounds o' boned-out Carcane meat
  come flyin' through the air
  an' landed smack right at my feet.
I untied the empty hide from off the holler log
  an' packed the Carcane meat inside,
  then drug it down the hill.
I left the bones an' skull up there,
  where you can see 'em still.

The boys in camp come out to greet me like a winner
  when they seen me draggin' in
  that Carcane meat for dinner.
But when the lads commenced to eat
  some claimed that it was painter meat,
  which was why it was so sweet,
  whilst others were prepared to swear
  'twarn't nothin' but a grizzly bear.
Them trappers who were Delaware
  declared the meat was dog,
  a treat they deem superior to any barnyard hog.
I myself was not prepared to say.
  They wouldn'a b'lieved me anyway.

              ร   ร   ร

Bitter Crick

As this book begins to wind down it's fitting that we hear just one more Jim Bridger yarn. At least he always said it was his; but even if it wasn't his originally, ol' Gabe ended up with most of the good stories from the glory days of the beaver trade, just because he lasted longer in the Rockies, and later in Missouri, where he returned to die, than most of his companyeros.

I need to mention here one of my continuing regrets. As we approach the end of the Twentieth Century I believe that it's a downright shame that we Americans have abandoned a lot of knowledge our grandfathers used to take for granted; and we've lost a lot of useful words, too. Take, for instance, the word alum, which is a traditional household chemical that causes drying, puckering, shriveling, and shrinking. Alum is still used nowadays for preserving pickles, but most folks don't can their own pickles anymore, so we've just about lost that useful word. A whole generation, or maybe two, doesn't know what alum is.

Well, that's enough complaining about lost language. Let's get back to the cookfire and a tall story called Bitter Crick.

Bitter Crick

I reckon that I've got a bellyful
  o' your sly smiles an' disbelievin' ways,
  your subtile accusations o' wilful fabrication,
  to last me for the rest of all my mortal days.
In spite of all my pledges an' my promises
  that what I say is jist as true as sacred Holy Writ,
  you're still a pack o' skepticizin', criticizin'
  fish-eyed Doubtin' Thomases!
I will admit that I've been known
  to maybe stray a bit from chapter, verse, an' letter,
  but that don't make no consequential nevermind
  about the fundamental truth of it.
All it does is make a worthwhile yarn
  perhaps a little better.
I ain't inclined to serve up no more tales o' mine.
You don't deserve no histories as fine
  as them I tell about.
Instead I'll 'cite you one from out
  of ol' Jim Bridger's life,
  a history as true as any steel you'll find
  in ev'ry kind o' good Green River skinnin' knife.
An' this I warrant that you know, jist as well as I
  — ever'body knows ol' Gabe, why hell!
  he surely wouldn't tell a lie!

Seems like ol' Gabe was scoutin' out
  some beaver-trappin' land for his brigade,
  come outen Pierre's in thirty-two.

'Twas late in fall an' all the ground was laden with
  a heavy fall o' snow.
They'd discovered a tall sugarloaf
  a-standin' all alone upon a great plateau,
  a sort o' solitary tower covered with a power of
  aspen, cottonwood, an' pine a-growin' thick,
  with broad an' gen'rous streams
  still flowin' quick an' showin' a sufficiency
  o' purely virgin' beaver sign.
Jim'd rode nigh halfway 'round that mount
  an' strode on snowshoes for more miles
  than he'd'a been o' mind to count.
The daylight it was wearin' thin
  an' Bridger reckoned 'twas high time
  to git on to his camp agin.
He tied his snowshoes on his horse
  an' set his course on his back trail.
He hadn't hardly gained a chain or two
  when Bridger spied a pack o' Grovant aborigines,
  a train o' braves an' kids an' squaws.
Big-belly Blackfoots was exac'ly what they was,
  an' sartinly still smartin' from
  the drubbin' that we gave 'em
  down at last summer's rendezvous.
Now Gabe he knew there warn't no mountain men
  a-standin' nigh to save him
  an' them Atsina braves had spied him
  jist about the time that he saw them.
  'Twarn't no time to hem an' haw.
  'Twas only time for savin' his own hide.
Them Atsina bucks begun to shout
  an' figgered that they had him treed.
Bridger hied his pony right about
  an' fairly lit a shuck, not trustin' none to luck,

jist bustin' loose an' lopin' out
  an' makin' trail, not stoppin' none to fight,
  jist hopin' he could keep his lead
  until the light begun to fail.
Jim high-tailed 'round the mountain,
  all the while a-countin' ev'ry step
  an' stride an' mile his pony pounded through the snow.
But for all the ridin' that he done,
  he couldn't seem to shake a one o' them Atsina braves,
  an' they was makin' better time than Gabe,
  seein' he was breakin' trail for them
  through all that drifted snow.
They was closin' on him steady an' there warn't
  no likely place to go an' hide.
Bridger he was nearly ready fer givin' up his ride
  an' makin' a last stand of it,
  when suddenly his pony rounded out
  the mountain an' begun a-runnin' down the other side.
Leastaways the track was leadin' back to camp,
  where Fitz an' Frapp an' ol' Gervais
  would surely light the welcome lamp
  and organize the trappers to provide
  a man-size helpin' of some hot an' hearty
  hospitality for all that yelpin'
  Blackfoot party ridin' hard upon his tail.
'Twas jist a momentary thought,
  for then he realized his horse was sure to fail.
Used up like he was, that pony couldn't run
  the distance that remained for gittin' back to camp.
Ol' Gabe begun to feel his armpits growin' damp.
His mouth was goin' dry.
His knees was meltin' all to jelly
  an' deep within his belly
  he felt the freezin' clamp o' cramp.

Jim's pony still was goin' halfway strong,
  showin' strain but runnin'
  with a long an' swingin' stride
  down along the mountainside,
  still leadin' that Atsina train a-stringin' out in back,
  when suddenly the track jist dropped away.
They busted through a thicket and afore
  ol' Gabe could yell a whoa,
  they crashed into a crick, a-splashin' and a-thrashin',
  an' fightin' jist to stay upright.
Then Jim he noticed that his pony warn't
  near as tuckered as he'd been
  an' that his own mouth was queerly puckered,
  his cheeks a-drawin' tight as skin upon an Injun drum.
'Twarn't no time to ponder what an' why,
  nor to wonder wherefore nor about how-come.
Gabe jist knew that what he had to do
  was gittin' out from where them Injuns was a-comin' from.
He kicked his pony up the bank,
  barely takin' time to thank his lucky stars
  for whatever gave his horse
  the gumption an' the extra force it took
  to keep ahead of all them Blackfoot bucks an' squaws
  who didn't care to let his hair
  remain precisely where it was.
Bridger raced on down the crick,
  stayin' deep within the bed,
  usin' ev'ry trick he knew to keep ahead,
  dodgin' arrow shafts an' lead,
  ridin' high an' light upon his horse's shoulders,
  stayin' nigh 'longside the watercourse
  an' cuttin' close to trees an' roots an' logs an' boulders,
  so's to cheat the Grovants' aim
  an' let ol' Casapy get back to whencesoever that he came.

Gabe was doin' all the things
  a righteous mountaineer had orter,
  when suddenly he realized
  his horse was growin' somewhat shorter!
His good ol' pony was most surely shriv'lin'!
An' once when he was swiv'lin' 'round,
  he found his moccasins was draggin' on the ground.
  That horse had lost a hand or two or three!
Ol' Gabe he tossed about within his memory
  an' then he recomembered how it was
  that pony had regained his legs
  an' then how he hisself had tasted rotten eggs
  an' how his lips commenced to pucker an' compress,
  jist like a prideful yankee gentleman
  all gussied up an' dressed in his best bib an' tucker.
Now Casapy he wasn't hardly never thick.
That is to say, Ol' Gabe, he hardly ever fumbled.
He tumbled to the truth right then.
  He'd stumbled through an alum crick!
'Twas then ol' Bridger felt his pony goin' lame.
'Twasn't any wonder, takin' in consideration
  all the rocky way they came.
  But thunder an' damnation!
No matter what your tribe or nation,
  I warrant you'd despaired of all salvation
  an' learned the stinkin' use o' fear,
  if you'd'a looked through Bridger's eyes right then
  an' seen that pony's feet a-drawin' up an' shrinkin',
  his tracks no bigger than a deer!
Now Gabe got down to facts an' bedrock thinkin'.
The Blackfoots they was gittin' near,
  their lead an' arrows still a-flittin' and a-plinkin'
  'round about the watercourse.
He realized he dassn't step onto that stinkin' alum ground,

else he hisself'd be a pint-size cripple, too,
  jist like his ever-shrinkin' horse.
He knew 'twas time he tried to make some tracks,
  but all the facts forbade him to skedaddle on afoot
  — until he recomembered that he'd tied
  his snowshoes on beside his saddle.
He lashed them snowshoes on real good, jumped off his horse,
  an' then begun to tramp as fast he could,
  runnin' down the canyon, back to camp.
The Injuns was by now unhorsed an' forced
  to foller him on foot, mad as hell and on the boil,
  — meanwhile a-shrinkin' jist a mite
  with ev'ry step they put upon that alum soil.
Ol' Bridger he kept goin' on,
  trampin' through that bitter snow
  with a kind of awful desperation,
  knowin' in his heart that ever' mile
  could be his last upon this footstool o' Creation.
He knew that he was strong, but Jim he warn't nobody's fool.
The distance back to camp was jist a mite too long to tramp.
It'd taken more'n half a day for him to ride
  not quite halfway around that butte,
  not stoppin' none to fight or shoot
  nor lookin' for a place to hide.
Jim paused a mite an' took another shot
  an' noticed that the motley lot
  o' Grovants was sure-enough a-gittin' smaller.
Last time he looked, he could'a swore,
  them heathens they was somewhat taller.
Them Injuns they was slippin' down inside o' their capotes,
  still turkey-gobblin' war cries in their throats,
  draggin' on their muskets an' their bows,
  but still they never quit their hobblin' through
  those alum-flavored snows.

Jim knew his strength was well-nigh spent
  an' he was less'n halfway home to camp,
    but mushin' down the mountainside he went,
    cussin' Injuns an' the cramp
      that felt like hard-boiled eggs inside his legs,
      still seekin' for the welcome lamp.
An' then he peeked around a rock
  an' saw his pards a-lazin' 'round the fire
    an' all the stock a-grazin' there,
    and ev'rythin' he could desire.
Gabe tried his best to give a shout,
  but nothin' very much come out.
Ol' Casapy was surely tuckered
  an' bound to give out purty soon.
He found his lips was purely puckered,
  his face all wrinkled like a prune.
Still, one thing was irritatin' Jim.
'Twas how he could miscalca'late
  the distance 'round the eastern side.
What'd occupied nigh half a day to ride
  he'd mushed afoot in somethin' less
  than hardly half that time.
An' then it come to him, jist like
  a thunderbolt from out the blue.
  The alum surely shrunk the distance, too!

Then when them pesky Grovants
  come roarin' 'round the rock,
    it had to be some kind o' mighty fearsome shock
    to find the whole brigade a-waitin' there,
    jist itchin' to collect their hair.
They turned their tails an' run back up the draw.
An' that's the very last o' them Jim Bridger ever saw.

But you can see 'em up there still
   upon the eastern side o' that there tower hill,
   a bunch o' little Blackfoots, no bigger than a child,
   nowheres near half-civilized,
   fact is, they're purely wild,
   crawlin' over roots an' logs an' ridin' ponies 'bout
   the size of Injun dogs, huntin' conies an'
   them sorry javelinos, them southern prairie hogs,
   an' settin' traps for trappers in them stinkin' alum bogs.

Ol' Gabe he smiled to see them Injuns run
   an' beat a wild retreat.
Then he begun to feel a pinchin' on his feet.
His snowshoes they was clinchin' up,
   not hardly bigger than his moccasins.
He shoved 'em in his possibles against a time
   he'd use 'em for some curin' frames
   for winter weasel skins.

So there you have the pure unvarnished truth,
   nothin' less an' nothin' more, without prevarication.
I hope an' pray you'll see your way
   to shore up an' perhaps restore my tarnished reputation.
Like I said before, cross my heart an' hope to die,
   ol' Gabe Bridger wouldn't lie!

                         ❧   ❧   ❧

Paradise

As the beaver trade drew to an end in the late 1830's, the signs of its demise were impossible to ignore. Beaver were scarce and the price of pelts had plummeted from their value during the glory days of the '20's, when three or four prime pelts could buy one of Jacob Hawken's better rifles in St. Louis. Naturally that was in St. Louis; in the mountains the price was considerably more dear, up to a thousand percent higher.

Mountaineers doubtless became aware of their own mortality as they saw their way of life and their treasured freedom slipping away. But let's listen to one of the old-timers tell it in his own way as he considers Paradise.

Paradise

Well, I come down here to celebrate
  another trappers' rendezvous,
  where Hoss Crick feeds the Seeds-kee-dee,
  but damn me if I didn't find
  a spate o' movers comin' through,
  thick as blowflies spilin' meat, upon their way to Oregon,
  behavin' like they lost their mind.
Why, they intend to drive their wagons
  clean acrost these Shinin' Mountains,
  with dairy cows, white womenfolk,
  an' young'uns past all countin'!
Jist yesterday I come to hear some greenhorn pilgrim tell
  a mover feller how the year's eighteen an' thirty-seven now
  — an' what a sorry year it's come to be!
The beaver market's mostly gone to hell
  an' plews an' meat are scanty as a city parson's charity.
Perhaps we should'a seen it comin',
  'cause last year's rendezvous
  was purely hummin' with a flock
  o' prodigies no beaver trapper ever knew.
'Twas quite a shock when Tom Fitzpatrick brung
  amongst us what we took to be a travelin' menagerie.
Bill Stewart was the first one that we see
  — an' though a Scottish lord he be,
  he's sure enough a grizzly-killer —
  come draggin' up to rendezvous
  an artist feller name o' Jacob Miller.

Then taggin' on behind 'em in a wagon
  there come a pair o' missionaries!
But all them foreign matters ain't precisely what
  plumb got the most of us unstrung —
  them preachers sure as hell had brung
  their dainty eastern wives along!
  White women at a rendezvous!
Sich a thing is dreadful wrong,
  I absolutely warrant you!
The one called Marcus Whitman the most of us recalled
  from rendezvous in thirty-five
  an' how he kept ol' Jim alive
  by diggin' out from Bridger's back a Blackfoot arrowhead.
An' when he said he marveled at
  jist why ol' Gabe warn't dead,
  ol' Bridger laughs an' shakes his head
  an' answers with a smile,
  "We're in the Rocky Mountains, Doc,
    an' here the meat don't spile!"
If I needed a sky pilot to guide me to the Promised Land,
  I reckon I'd pick Whitman,
  'cause he's got sand enough to be a proper mountain man.
T'other parson's name was Spauldin',
  lean an' crabby, pinched an' baldin'.
Right off he fixed his eye on me
  an' never missed a chance to tell
  me I was headin' straight for hell.
Whitman's wife Narcissa was purely ev'ry trapper's dream
  an' whilst she stayed amongst us
  that lady surely reigned supreme.
Copper blonde she was, complexion like a peach,
  but Narcissa she was far beyond
  a beaver trapper's reach.
But then her friend Eliza made the most of us to recollect

white women in the States an' how them females mostly was
— which made us all appreciate the more
　our dusky Injun squaws.
Cap'n Stewart brung a store o' fancy food an' foreign drink,
　enough to make a body think
　　that back in all the settlements an' most o' Europe, too,
　there couldn't possibly be more
　than what he brung to rendezvous.
His sarvints set theirselves to spread an absolute galore
　o' Spanish brandy, Guinness ale, an' spicy Polish hams,
　　sarved up with fancy English bread
　　all slathered with presarves an' jams,
　　an' gobs o' steamin' corn beef briskets,
　　pecks o' crumbly Scottish biscuits,
　　an' smoky little oysters from a tin,
　　washed down with French champagne,
　which, for drinkin' serious, I judge to be a trifle thin.
After I had et an' drunk a more'n full sufficiency
　o' Stewart's hospitality, I props m'self agin a tree
　　an' smokes a pipe or two or mebbe three
　　an' gen'rally relaxes.
Then sure as death an' hell an' taxes
　here comes Parson Spauldin' headin' straight for me.
He hunkers down an' stares into my eyes
　an' asks me don't I realize
　　if I don't mend my sinful ways
　　I won't get into Paradise?
'Bout then I'm feelin' kind o' sassy,
　so I asks him, bold an' brassy as ye please,
　　why should I foller where he's leadin'
　　an' what's it like in that'ere Eden?
Right off I realized I'd played into his hand
　an' he begun to lecture me on all he knew concernin'
　　Heaven, Paradise, an' Promised Land,

extracted from his Good Book learnin'.
'Bout all it 'mounted to was findin' peace
   and ice-cold happiness an' sittin' on a cloud
   an' playin' harps amongst a crowd
   o' pious pilgrims singin' psalms the rest of all eternity.
I reckoned 'twarn't no place for me.
Sich a barren place would hafta be
   — the plain, unvarnished truth to tell —
   for me or any mountain man a damn sight worse'n hell!
One thing that truly got my goat
   was when that preacher said, to my complete surprise,
   there ain't no horses 'lowed in that'ere Paradise.
   Well, I say that stick don't float!
Now, how could any worthwhile God create
   that handsome critter what contains
   a passel o' those virtues that
   all the parsons claim to venerate so much,
   like bravery an' patience, trustworthiness
   an' honesty an' loyalty an' such,
   then turn Hisself about an' shut
   that self-same critter out?
An' here's another thought, besides.
A truly wise Great Spirit knows, even in His far-off Paradise,
   a man'd be a fool to walk
   when there's a horse that he can ride!

The more I thought about it, the more certainly I knew
   that Heaven is the lastin' place
   where all your pleasant dreams come true.
So I set myself to cogitatin' on the marvels that are waitin'
   when I draw my final breath an' shed this mortal life
   an' go to meet my death.
I reckon I can find my way without no missionary.
He ain't been there, no more'n me.

Why, mountaineers can carry on
  an' find a proper trail out to the Western Sea!
I guarantee I won't get lost
  an' that I'll find that final stream
  an' that, somehow, I'll get acrost.
To me, it jist seems right an' proper
  that mountain men who've spent their days
  a-trappin' beaver plews to make
  some city feller's fancy topper
  had truly oughter cross some water after their demise
  whilst trav'lin on their way to Paradise.
And on the other side I see a wide an' grassy plain
  with flocks of antelopes a-sunnin'
  an' black with buffler herds a-runnin' far an' wide,
  drummin' on the ground an' makin' sich a sound
  to make you think o' summer thunder.
An' over yonder there's a plumb galore
  of all my companyeros gone under years before.
Of all the things to make my Paradise complete
  the sweetest thing'll be to greet
  those rough an' ready mountain men
  an' be amongst my friends again.
'Sides buffler cows an' antelope,
  I see amongst the trees the deer
  as thick as prairie grass an' gangs o' wapitis.
The streams are runnin' cold an' pure
  an' teemin' with prime beaver plews.
That's surely all the happiness
  a mountaineer can ever use.
Then pushin' up beside each berry bush an' tree,
  defyin' all o' Nature's laws,
  I see a wealth o' first-rate prime tobacco chaws
  an' pokin' up betwixt 'em, there's even more for smokin'.
An' springs o' pure metheglin, a mixture of sweet honey mead

an' top-notch trader's booze,
come oozin' out from ev'ry hilly rise
the kind o' drink a trapper'd need
to guarantee his Paradise.
An' there ain't like to be no bugs in any heaven of my makin',
  'cause if there ain't no kind
o' creepy, crawlin' critters there,
  'tain't likely that you're apt to find
no thievin', stealin', plunder-takin',
  cricket-eatin', ever-cheatin'
Paiute Injuns where I intend myself to be
  the balance of eternity.
But on the other hand, I reckon there'll be a band
  o' pesky Blackfoot Injuns there,
residin' in my Promised Land,
  'cause my eternal bliss depends
on sorry critters sich as these.
If a man don't have no enemies
  — well, he can't hardly recognize his friends!
'Course, I warrant jist the same,
  them Blackfoot bucks'll be
blind of, at the very least, one eye
  an' more'n jist a trifle lame.
That's jist the men, I hope ye see.
For me, no bunch o' women ever was
  as handsome as the Blackfoot squaws.

Imaginin' my Paradise ain't no tough chore for me.
You pilgrims, swing your head around
  an' tell me what you see.
Don't need no harps to realize the Heaven of my dreams.
That's Heaven right before your eyes
  an' it's jist what it seems.
There's organs boomin' in the pines

and angels sing in canyon winds.
  They're laughin' in the streams.
Don't need no cold white marble halls,
  nor streets o' gold, nor crystal fountains.
  I'll take for mine jist what ye see
  in these here Rocky Mountains!
There's so much beauty hereabouts
  that I will never get my fill.
Even Eden couldn't shine beside these Shinin' Hills!

But when all o' that is said an' done
  the one important thing in Paradise'll be
  jist feelin' the Great Spirit all around
  an' all the time, in ev'ry rock an' tree
  an' comin' from the ground,
  like happens oncet'awhile upon a starry night
  or mebbe jist at dawn,
  a feelin' that plumb fills you up,
  but all too soon, it's gone.
An' then, may be, I'll never see that ideal Paradise.
I don't pretend to be so wise to see beyond my death.
Perhaps I'll draw my final breath
  an' watch the earth grow dim
  an' drift into eternal sleep
  an' what was me will be no more
  than some ol' aspen's cast-off limb
  left rottin' on the ground.
But if that's so, be sure, my friends
  this mountain man will sartinly be still around.

You'll see me in the grass an' trees
  an' ev'ry breeze will blow a tiny mote o' me
  to each tall mountain peak.
Then I'll come a-driftin' down

some icy-cold high mountain creek,
feedin' Rocky Mountain trout,
until some eagle swoops an' scoops him out
— an' so it goes, and on I'll go,
helpin' plants an' critters grow.
An' if by chance I have a soul an' if I ever learn to pray,
  I'll ask the Father-of-it-All jist to let this critter stay
  amongst these Rocky Mountains, never more to stray.
An' now I reckon that you see
  these Shinin' Hills have always been
  an' certainly will always be
  the perfect Paradise for all such men as me.

                    ॐ   ॐ   ॐ

Knots

Most of a mountain man's most valuable possessions weren't carried in his possibles bag or on his saddle. Those were his knowledge, experience, and skills — the hard-won savvy that often meant the difference between success and failure, or, much more important, life and death. Among those skills one of the most important was a knowledge of Knots.

Knots

There's lots o' things a mountaineer
  had oughta know afore he goes
  a-traipsin' off to these here Shinin' Hills
  — but of all the skills a trapper's got
  amongst the most important is knowin' how to tie a knot.
There's knots we use to make a noose
  when settin' out a rabbit snare
  or buildin' traps for grizzly bear —
  an' those we use for hobbles
  an' puttin' horses on a tether.
'Course ev'ry trapper knows the knack
  o' tyin' diamond hitches,
  which is the knot we use to tie a horse's pack
  so's to keep it all together.
There's got to be a hunnerd knots o' wide an' sundry uses,
  all kinds o' twists an' bends an' reefs,
  hitches, squares, Turk's heads, an nooses.
Knots are jist as useful as
  your rifle gun or skinnin' knife.
I'll tell you now jist how
  knowin' knots once saved my life.

One day in spring o' thirty-one,
  when I had got my trappin' done,
  I trotted back to camp along the Seeds-kee-dee,
  totin' three prime beaver pelts
  and, natcherly, my rifle gun,

when, up ahead, I chanced to see a deer.
I stop an' aim an' shoot,
  but 'fore the smoke has time to clear,
  I hear an fearsome rattle ringin' in my ear.
I swing m'self around an' see
  a most hellacious sarpint hangin' from a tree.
At least two rods o' snake there was,
  fair thirty feet an' more,
  coiled around a pine tree limb,
  his tail a-scrapin' on the forest floor,
  huge rattles lookin' like a string
  o' dried-out Injun gourds,
  an' fangs a-hangin' down like swords
  from out his gapin' maw
  — an' I was surely movin' towards
  my judgment by Eternal Law.
I reached down for my powder horn
  an' he r'ared up to strike at me.
I knew as sure as I was born, I'd better let my rifle be.
No matter where I put my foot
  that snake maintained his range on me.
He follered ev'ry move I made,
  his eyes as big as lantrens,
  unblinkin' in the light or shade.
He backed if I eased forward an' follered if I backed —
  an' if I stepped to left or right,
  he kept his wicked head on me, still threatenin' to bite.
A thought occurred that seemed to me
  to be worthwhile the chancin',
  since Mister Snake appeared to be enamored of our dancin'.
I sidle slow jist two steps right.
He rattles once but doesn't bite an' follers where I lead,
  his beady eyes plumb filled with greed.
I stepped up on a rock behind me.

He raised up, too, so as to find me,
  then backed an' ducked as I stepped down.
I circled once, then made a dainty curlicue or two,
  cavortin' like a circus clown.
The snake he does exac'ly as I do,
  crossin' plumb acrost hisself an' droopin' when I droop,
  an' finally he sticks his head plumb through a loop.
I picked this moment for to make a backward somersault.
He shoots his head straight out to strike.
  What happened next was sure my fault!
He stopped as like as if as he was shot.
  He'd clinched hisself down to that limb,
  tied in a perfect bowline knot!
That sarpint roared an' then he cried
  an' then committed suicide.
I don't believe it's what he meant.
  It was more like an accident.
He screamed an' hollered, then he'd shriek,
  makin' that whole tree to creak,
  then sank his fangs into the limb
  — an' that was sure the end o' him!
The wood swole up, I truly swear,
  an' choked that critter fair an' square!

My pards an' me was pleased to take
  the hide o' that hellacious snake
  an' make a thirty-foot canoe
  for floatin' all our beaver plew
  on down to summer rendezvous!

ॐ   ॐ   ॐ

Oregon

No matter how content a man might be in his new-found home, his place of birth, or descent, is still a matter of pride, especially if he's Irish. Even native-born mountain men were but a generation or two removed from Europe, from which their families had emigrated to America. The pride they felt in their origins was especially strong in the Irish, who were generally despised and denigrated on America's eastern seaboard. So when they came to the mountains to pursue the trapper's trade and were judged solely on their individual merit, the pride they felt in being Irish occasionally got somewhat out of hand, especially in their stories.

The following tale might have been told beside a Rocky Mountain campfire by Tom "Broken Hand" Fitzpatrick, who emigrated from Ireland to America as a very young man and who proved himself any man's equal in the fur trade, finally becoming a major partner in the Rocky Mountain Fur Company and, later, after the fur trade went bust, Superintendent of Indian Affairs in the West.

It should be mentioned here that scholars have long disagreed about the naming of the Territory of Oregon. All scholarly explanations have generally been dismissed as mere conjecture and the matter remains to this day a philological mystery.

One more thing. I truly hope that I won't offend any grizzly bears or their Animal Rights defenders by any remarks contained in this story. Such references seek only to reflect and depict the attitudes of the mountain men and are not necessarily my own.

But now let's get back to the fire and listen to Fitz regale his comrades with what really happened in the naming of Oregon.

Oregon

Sure an' I have listened to enough an' more o' fancy tales
  concernin' how you mountain men
  are always after blazin' trails
  to miracles o' boilin' fountains,
  burnin' rivers, lakes, an' streams
  an' even mountains made o' glass
  — an' how 'twas Jedediah Smith
  who was first to tread the path
  through what we're callin' now South Pass
  — an' Seamus Bridger bein' first to take
  a briny bath in Great Salt Lake.
Faith, to hear ye talk, a body'd think
  the Great Creator of It All
  would hesitate to yawn or blink
  without receivin' by-your-leave
  from the sorry likes o' you,
  whene'er you're spinnin' trapper's yarns
  in winter camp or rendezvous.
There's some amongst us mountaineers
  who'll happily endure the worst
  o' hunger an' the tortures of
  the desert's murd'rous thirst
  if only they can get from here
  to some unknown wherever first.
An' there's others like to burst their shirts
  with altogether overweenin' pride
  if they can be the first to climb

some undiscovered mountainside.
We're here to harvest beaver hides
an' not to brag on bein' first!

Still, I've been wond'rin' if I durst to tell
  the tale of how it came about
  that Oregon first got its name.
It may be you won't agree, but all the same,
  the namin' o' that territory makes a fascinatin' story.
An' hearin' all the details o' that tale
  is sure to warm the heart of ev'ry Gael
  an' add a wreath or two to Erin's glory.

'Twas long before Tom Jefferson
  made his captains sally forth,
  explorin' lands far to the west
  an' then a-trav'lin' somewhat north,
  when Meriwether Lewis was still list'nin' for
  the ringin' of his schoolmarm's bell
  an' Billy Clark was jist a-learnin' how to spell.
'Twas then that Teague O'Reagan
  bade farewell to Erin's Sod an' traveled to America,
  trustin' most in his right arm
  — the rest he left to God.
He'd had a bellyful o' Sassenachs and England's Cruel Red
  an' Tyrant Georgie's bleedin' tax,
  feedin' off of Irishmen
  'til they was better off when dead.

O'Reagan was a giant of a man,
  with hair an' beard a flamin' red,
  a brow o' sev'ral span,
  Killarney eyes that knew no dread,
  a mouth upturned with laughter,

and after never tellin' lies, 'tis said,
shoulders broad as Liffey's stream an' narrow at the hip,
with arms as strong as chapel beams or masts upon a ship.

When Teague O'Reagan's ship arrived
on Boston's rocky shore,
he found the Yankee colonies a-fightin' bloody war,
chasin' out the Redcoats an' tax-collectors, too
— so natcherly naught else would do
but Teague O'Reagan joinin' up
an' battlin' 'gin the British, too.
He threw his might into the fight.
He gave his Irish all.
There's naught to please an Irishman like mixin' in a brawl.
But after he had killed or maimed a regiment or two,
Teague bethought himself 'twas time
to finish what he'd come to do.
So when he seen George Washington
had the matter well in hand,
he said, "Now I'll be leavin' you
an' scout about this charmin' land."

O'Reagan set his course upon the settin' sun
and ere the first fortnight was done,
he gazed upon the Western Sea an' found it to his likin',
well-worth the time an' effort required for his hikin'.
The land about him pleased him, too,
an' nothin' else, it seemed, would do
except to claim this charmin' place
in honor o' the Celtic race.
The hills an' vales were lush an' green,
not the greenest he had seen, by any means,
but still the best he'd seen in all his trav'lin west.
This western land, please understand,

can ne'er compare with Ireland,
for nothin' on this earth beguiles
  like Irish Galway's Aran Isles
  whene'er those sea-borne clouds are kissed
  by a delicious mornin' mist.
  There is no mortal sight, I'm thinkin',
  that fills the heart like drinkin' in
  sweet Erin's em'rald hills.
At first O'Reagan thought to call
  this new-discovered plot o' ground somethin' like New Erin,
  but then he found another name an' liked it best of all.
Soon you could hear 'im swearin' —
  "Sure, you can take my space in Heaven
  an' damn me for a pagan
  if I won't name this darlin' place the Nation of O'Reagan!"
Upon that oath he staked his claim
  to all the land that to this day
  bears the proud O'Reagan name,
  corrupted more'n somewhat by the heathen Injun tongue,
  but in the hearts of Irishmen
  Teague's fame remains forever young.

But gainin' fame was only part
  of all the jobs O'Reagan meant to do.
So for a start he set about amassin' gobs o' beaver plew.
Each stream of ev'ry mountain teemed
  with beaver dams past countin'
  an' yet to Teague it surely seemed
  that trappin' each an' ev'ry one
  would be a process much too slow.
So O'Reagan dammed Columbia!
He blocked the river's flow an' backed it up until
  the water flooded ev'ry hill
  an' washed them beavers down below.

Then Teague he broke the dam an' seined out ev'ry castor.
  O'Reagan, once he set his mind, could be
  a natural disaster!
An' you can see the traces still,
  reachin' clear to Blackfoot land,
  the marks o' that almighty lake
  O'Reagan set hisself to make
  — the rosy stripes upon yon hills
  an' diff'rent colors in the sand.

His fortune made, Teague faced the task
  o' ladin' all his furs back east
  to trade for all the precious gold
  an Irishman could ask.
It took all day for Teague to build a mighty cargo dray,
  full forty rod in length it was an' nearly half as wide,
  the wheels as tall as miller's stones, twenty to a side.
Big as it was, it barely held each an' ev'ry beaver pelt,
  a tribute to the trappin' skill o' Teague the hardy Celt.
For haulin' o' that juggernaut
  he broke to yoke fair forty span
  o' buffler bulls, for nothin' pulls
  like buffler bulls, once he had 'em taught.
An' then he caught a grizzly sow
  to keep them bufflers movin' smart
  — from time to time to make 'em halt
  an' then again to make 'em start.
An' so they set out for the East,
  to-wards the risin' sun,
  O'Reagan feelin' satisfied that half his work was done.
  But back along the ocean shore
  the Injuns mourned O'Reagan,
  so they went to carvin' pagan
  totem poles in memory o' Teague,

revered by them forevermore.

Whilst they was goin' to the East,
  Teague started growin' sentimental
  concernin' all the virtues of his helpmeet grizzly sow,
  which helps in the explainin' how
  them two was entertainin' one another in the blankets
  ere the journey was half-done.
It started off with keepin' warm,
  but soon, as Teague hisself'd say,
  it was "any port'll do ye when you're ridin' out a storm"
  — although the buggered Sassenachs
  might call sich things "bad form."
O'Reagan had no doubt his Irish seed would stick,
  so when he bade his grizzly sow Godspeed,
  he did like any self-respectin' Mick
  an' told his ursine paramour
  to raise the children Cath-o-lic.

Sure, I reckon that I see about this camp
  a few who bear O'Reagan's stamp,
  more'n one bone-ugly, halfway-human critter
  that likely is a product of
  that grizzly sow's unnat'ral litter!

Arrivin' in New York, Teague O'Reagan sold
  his furs for eighty hogsheads, each one brimful o' gold.
He bought hisself a sailin' ship huge enough to hold
  the fortune that had come to hand,
  then set his course for Ireland.
Once there he knelt an' kissed the Sod
  an' bein' sich a pious Celt, he gave his thanks to God.
Then off he went to County Meath
  an' journeyed to the vale beneath

the hill that holds famed Tara's Hall,
  the seat of ancient Irish kings.
Right then O'Reagan bought it all,
  the castle an' the cattle, the village an' the vale,
  an' decked those halls with furnishings
  befittin' Erin's ancient kings,
  which swelled the pride of ev'ry Gael.
He swept out all the Sassenachs
  an' paid King Georgie's bloody tax
  with pocket change, for he was rich
  beyond all mortal countin' —
  an' gen'rous to all Irishmen as some eternal fountain.
Ere long he wed a princess of ancient Irish blood
  an' they have Celtic sons enough
  to make ye call old Tara's Hall O'Reagan's Irish stud.
For all I know, he reigns there still,
  a king, in truth, on Tara's Hill.

So there it is, the plain unvarnished story
  o' Teague O'Reagan's everlastin' glory
  an' how, in truth, he came to name
  that darlin' territory.
An' if ye wish that I refrain from callin' you a pagan,
  jist please don't call it Oregon.
  It's best pronounced O'Reagan!

                     ☙   ☙   ☙

Let Me Cross Over

I doubt that any mountain man ever wrote a religious hymn, although it's reasonable to assume that a few trappers, Jedediah Smith certainly among them, probably sang traditional hymns now and then.

But supposing that a mountain man were to write a hymn, I believe that it would be both secular and somewhat reflective of Native American spiritual attitudes and that it would sound something like this one, *Let Me Cross Over*.

Let Me Cross Over (a hymn)

Let me cross over to the other shore
  and be with my comrades
  in peace evermore.
Let me cross over.
  Show me the way.
It's time that I go to pay what I owe
  on my Judgment Day.
Let me cross over.
  Show me the ford.
Let me lie in the shade of the trees
  on the other shore
  and know lasting peace for time evermore.

Let me cross over
  where grass still grows high,
  where buffalo thunder
  and land's not plowed under,
  where hearts are as pure and serene
  as the clean prairie sky.
I won't have to walk there.
  I know I can ride,
  for my faithful horses
   have crossed to that side
  — and my old companions
   all wait on that shore.
Just let me cross over
  and greet them once more.

Oh, let me cross over to that other shore
  and be with my comrades
  in peace evermore.
Let me cross over.
  Show me the way.
It's time that I go to pay what I owe
  on my Judgment Day.
Let me cross over.
  Show me the ford.
Let me lie in the shade of the trees
  on that other shore
  and know lasting peace for time evermore.

                                    ঌ   ঌ   ঌ

Last Rendezvous

And then, nobody was quite sure why, it was all over. The wonderful, free, unfettered life was gone beaver! Plews were scarce and even if you could trap enough beaver to make a bale or two, the market was gone, drowned in the tides of changing fashion. London fops were wearing silk hats now and the glory times were drawing to a close. Beaver would never shine again! Every mountain man knew it, although few would admit it at first.

The last big rendezvous was held in 1837 at Henry's Fork on the Seeds-kee-dee, Green River, but even there the death rattle of the beaver trade could be heard above the tinny ring of banjos, the fiddles, and the beat of Indian drums. By 1840 it was no more. The shinin' times had lasted less than twenty years.

Some of the mountain men drifted down to Taos, but things were hardly better there; others returned to the settlements; and some became guides for west-bound settlers or scouts for the Army. A lot of them simply disappeared into the mountains, living alone or with the Indians. But no matter which choice they made, all of them knew that none of them would ever be so completely free again.

Here is how one of those old hivernants might have told it, if you and he were leaning back and spinning yarns at his Last Rendezvous.

Last Rendezvous

Joe Walker's gone to Californy now
  an' most of all the rest o' that hard an' horny crew
  have made a meager best of all the beaver runnin' out
  by guidin' eager pilgrims to the Promised Land of Oregon.
Somehow it don't seem right to me
  to see a man sell off the only freedom that
  any man in history has known,
  by showin' clerks an' farmers the way to land that man
  was never meant to plow an' till.
They'll kill off all the game
  an' maim the spirit of the land!
They'll overflow the mountains
  an' turn the prairies into sand!
They'll pray to God for rain an' say
  that they can't live without it —
  but when the heavens open up an' pour
  they'll roar an' jist complain about it!
  I know them bacon-eaters!
I lived amongst 'em 'fore I come out in twenty-two,
  crowdin' one another somethin' fierce
  an' scrabblin' on their measly farms,
  scorchin' in the sun an' losin' crops
  to drouths an' hails.
They're always singin' psalms an' churchin'
  ev'ry Sabbath Day an' criticizin'
  — when they ain't busy buildin' jails!
  They like to call it civilizin'!

I knew it couldn't never be the kind o' life for such as me.

When I come out in twenty-two,
　life held no promise, only threats.
So like a lot of other men right then,
　I came up the Big Missourah
　without a backward glance an' no regrets.
This side o' the Muddy,
　where the Tetons offer up themselves
　to Injun gods I'll never know,
　a man's as free as he could ever wish to be.
We traveled on a keelboat on up the High Missourah —
　haulin' on a cordelle rope until your shoulder's raw,
　polin' in the shallows, strainin' on an oar,
　washin' city stink out of your nose,
　an' drainin' laws an' manners from your craw,
　drinkin' in the clean Missourah air,
　an' thinkin', mebbe sometimes, of a pretty squaw
　waitin' somewheres up the river
　that no man, 'cept an Injun, ever saw.
Lyin' out at sunset on the deck,
　head restin' on my hands behind my neck,
　I heard the curlews call
　an' watched a lazy heron flappin'
　slowly toward the settin' sun.
I knew that I'd be right for trappin',
　livin' off the land with jist my beaver traps
　an' knife an' gun.
Lyin' lazy with the sun a-plungin'
　from the hazy western sky,
　streakin' clouds a rich vermilion,
　like an Injun wearin' paint,
　a million eager thoughts overflowed my brain
　— an' I knew that I'd be stayin'

somewhere near to here until the day I die.

I trapped for Andrew Henry first,
  but after time I raised a thirst to try it on my own.
Oh, he an' Ashley they was square enough, I dare to say,
  but there's somethin' real important lackin'
  when it's another feller's beaver plews you're packin'.
I figgered that I couldn't shine
  'less all the chances that I took
  an' all the gains I made or lost were mine.
Still, I learned my trade with Andy,
  gettin' handy with a knife an' gun
  an' makin' beaver set, lettin' instinct dominate
  when thinkin's much too slow to save your life
  the day you come upon a grizzly bear
  or some Injun out to lift your hair.
I'd got the knack o' livin' 'thout bread or salt or greens
  or passin' fault to someone else
  or ever packin' blame myself.
I learned to live on meat.
I shot my game an' reckoned I'd become
  a mountaineer complete an' proper,
  trappin' beaver for some London dandy's topper.

I reckon that I've knowed 'em all, or most o' them —
  there wasn't but a thousand mountain men at most,
  from the brown Missourah to the blue Pacific coast.
I've froze my arse in beaver ponds
  with Walker an' Hugh Glass,
  afore he got it from the Rees up on the Yellerstone.
The best o' them are rotting bones,
  scattered by the wolves, picked clean by magpies,
  from the Seeds-kee-dee on up to the Yellerstone,
  Gallatin an' Jefferson an' Platte,

an' all the streams that feed the Big Missourah,
  flowin' brave men's blood into the Mississip,
  then goin' clean to New Orleans.
I listened to young Jedediah Smith preachin' 'gin the sins
  of over-reachin' that what's right for men to have an' do.
Too bad we didn't pay no mind, 'cause what he tried to say
  might'a stopped the doin's
  that each of us today must answer to.
He sounded like a prophet,
  for all his greasy buckskins an' his crazy bear-clawed eye
  — an' through the fire's dancin' light,
  I saw an' heard him for an honest man
  and in my heart I knew that he was right.

The fall o' twenty-seven, as near as I can figger,
  I threw in with a nigger mountain man.
  Jim Beckwith was his name.
Oh, he was a hoss! An' game?
Didn't know the use o' callin' no man boss.
He proved to me that, black or red or white,
  all righteous mountain men arc jist about the same.
I reckon that I earned my share o' beaver plews that year,
  but what I learned from Jim,
  the season that we stayed up there,
  I never could repay to him.
He taught me how to look an' listen
  an' all the things you oughter do so's to keep your hair.
When he'd teach, he didn't preach.
He'd show you what you had to know,
  if you hoped to see next rendezvous
  down on the Seeds-kee-dee.
  'Twas mighty like a christenin' for me.

An' sometimes in the winter,

shoulders propped agin an aspen trunk,
smokin' our tobacco mixed with willer bark,
sittin' by the flicker o' the fire gnawin at the dark,
he'd talk o' freedom like as if it was a liquor
that nearly made him drunk.
He'd say that even Blackfoots
could never strike the fear in him
he'd known afore he come out here
— that winter snows an' snakes an' bear
an' goin' dry an' hungry never could compare
with the misery a mortal knows
if he ain't completely free.
'Twas Jim who pointed out to me
that only mountain men are free
— the only men who ever were in all o' history.
Sure, Beckwith was a nigger,
but sometimes I wonder if he warn't
a bigger, whiter, wiser, better man than me.

In springtime when the beaver plews
was runnin' thin an' poor,
we packed our bales an' made our way
down narrow mountain trails,
until we come to prairies stretchin'
far an' wide, with elk an' deer
an' antelope an' buffler past recall.
We made our winter meat to hide in caches 'gainst the time
we'd climb the mountain trails in fall.

Then it come about at rendezvous,
some men were talkin' plans about the West
an' asked if we would come along.
I had some strong an' private business of my own
concernin' a young Injun lass

an' said that I would hafta pass.
But Jim was burnin' for the West.
I said he'd prob'ly had the best o' me
  an' told him to go on alone.
His grip was honest, firm, an' strong
  that final time he shook my hand.
He reined his horse around, then he was gone.
  I reckoned I had knowed a man.

The years slipped by like buffler filin' down a draw.
  I made my way to Bent's an' Touse an' Santa Fe
  an' saw the Great Salt Lake, made trade
  with Injuns all acrost the West,
  but still I'll take these mountains
  for the best that I have seen.
When they commence to green in spring —
  well, there ain't hardly anythin' I'd rather see
  than springtime on the Seeds-kee-dee
  an' knowin' that you're comin' to
  another trappers' rendezvous!

Christamighty! it was fun to see them Injun ponies run,
  lettin' off your gun
  an' feelin' solid horse betwixt your knees!
Trappers yellin' altogether somethin' sinful,
  like they was a bunch o' Sioux or Rees,
  long hair an' eagle feathers flyin',
  like they're dyin' for a skinful of
  the rotgut whiskey that the bourgeois sold,
  sweepin' into camp an' wakin' sleepin' dogs,
  jumpin' over logs an' dodgin' 'round
  the Injun lodges, ridin' bold, an' froze for company,
  the sound an' sight of all those old familiar faces,
  kickin' over traces, haulin' back to howl,

spoilin' for a fight, an' gettin' boiled as any owl!

Tradin' with the bourgeois never seemed to take much time.
He'd hem an' haw a bit, but he'd pay a man fair prices
  if the beaver that you packed was prime.
  That was the long an' short of it.
You think this is a rendezvous?
Hell! I been to some'd make two or three o' this'n!
Men playin' hand an' bettin' hard-won beaver plews
  in prime condition
  on a crazy guess on where the pebble was,
  not mindin' if they won or lost,
  jist happy bein' in amongst their kind
  an' findin' some familiar face,
  some dear ol' hoss you'd near forgot,
  givin' him a grizzly hug
  an' dancin' quick an' hot with liquor
  that you ain't had a chance to taste for nigh on to a year.
We played like kids at tug-o'-war an' shootin' at a mark.
Then after dark you'd go paradin' in
  your brand-new beaded buckskins,
  fringes flappin' in the breeze
  to set the Injun dogs a-yappin',
  sportin' moccasins with quills that run up to your knees,
  an' tradin' bright red blankets with the chiefs
  for beddin' pretty squaws
  — some amongst the Rees so white you'd almost think they was.

I remember that first rendezvous
  that Gen'ral Ashley brought me to
  in twenty-five, here on the Seeds-kee-dee.
If I should close my eyes right now,
  I could almost see, like it's alive,
  the cookin' fires burnin' quakin' asp,

the smoke a-risin' like an eagle feather,
'til it's lost amongst the trees,
a Yankee trader's banjo ringin',
a spotted horse a-frettin' at his tether,
the songs the mountain men are singin',
mixin' with the rasp an' hammer on a pony's feet,
the yammerin' o' Bannock Injun kids,
the smell o' cookin' meat,
the taste o' fresh tobacco smoke,
a bunch o' trappers gettin' drunk an' tellin' jokes,
an' laughter floatin' on the summer air.
Yes, it was awful good back there.

Then, after eatin', with your belly full
  o' buffler ribs an' hump an' marrow bone,
  an' takin' time for meetin' with a score or more o' men
  to smoke an' drink an' yarn 'bout gettin' rich,
  you'd itch to jump into the rendezvous again.
We'd go to swappin' trade cloth, paint, an' beads
  for Injun women's moccasins an' shirts
  — an' 'fore long, for liftin' Injun women's skirts.
Some o' those squaws'd laugh
  an' chaff you, makin' fun o' white men's ways,
  — but some'd make you think o' them
  through many winter nights an' days.
Some'd lie with legs widespread,
  like they was gutshot, mostly dead
  — but some'd rise to meet your thrust,
  laughin' like they're fit to bust!
An' sometimes, if she gave you more than she had sold,
  she'd hold you tight an' warm through all the night
  an' keep you from the cold
  that creeps into your mind betimes
  an' shared some of your secret thoughts

that you had never told.

Did I ever fall in love?
You bet your powder horn an' ball I did!
An Injun girl who had an eye as soft
  an' brown an' liquid as a beaver she.
Arapaho she was, as straight an' tall
  as aspens growin' in amongst the pines.
It took some doin's, but I made her mine
  — an' whilst she lived she owned the better part o' me.
  There's times an' circumstances when
  even a young mountain man don't mind
  if he ain't completely free.

It's eighteen an' thirty-seven now
  an' things jist ain't the same
  down here along the Seeds-kee-dee.
They're callin' it Green River nowadays
  an' more'n jist the name has changed.
Somehow it don't feel right to me no more!
It's less a rendezvous than it is a sort o' country store.
Why, you can drink a beaver plew in half a swaller!
The price o' pelts has gone to hell!
They tell me Englishmen an' Frogs've gone
  to wearin' toppers made o' silk
  an' that the beaver market's holler as a rotted log!
It's mebbe jist as well, 'cause all the beaver are
  purty nearly done.
It's jist like Jedediah said to us a hunnerd times,
  we've over-reached ourselves!
We've thinned the buffler somethin' fierce
  an' shot off all the deer 'round here.
  The beaver are all gone. God knows what else!
Hell! I ain't complainin' 'bout

the buffler an' the beaver runnin' out.
It's freedom that a mountain man
  can never hope to live without!
Sure, I admit we wasted a tremenjous lot
  o' buffler, wapiti, an' deer, but if you ever tasted
  fleece fat an' hump an' ribs, fresh shot,
  you'd'a done it, too.
'Sides, who'd've ever thought to fear
  that so much game could ever possibly run out?
Nowadays there ain't much game a-roamin' hereabouts,
  but 'fore I go to eatin' pork,
  I allow that I would rather do without!

I'm gettin' on to forty now
  an' the rheumatism that creeps in
  from wadin' in a thousand icy beaver ponds
  is slowin' up my gait.
There's some my age that's gone to keepin' store,
  workin' for a wage,
  an' waitin' on the trade that's movin' west
— but I'll be damned if I was made
  for counter-jumpin'! An' what's more,
  I'll be double-damned if I ever lift a hand
  to help a single wagon wheel
  roll acrost this mountain land!
'Fore I go to humpin' pilgrims through the Pass,
  like sneaky little Carson an' his band o' guides,
  I guess I'll take my chances with the Rees,
  the ones who scalped that tough ol' hoss Hugh Glass.

'Sides, it's time I set my trail stick headin' south.
Meat's still thick an' plenty down around the Forks
  an' I got a son amongst the 'Rapaho,
  if the white men's pox ain't rubbed him out.

Yes, it's time I go an' show him what he needs to be a man.
Reckon I can live without
  these movers crawlin' in amongst us from the East.
I reckon that I done at least my share
  o' liftin' hostile Injun hair — an' kept my own so far.
But even so, a man can build
  a certain grudgin' admiration for the braves
  of all the redskin nations.
Leastaways amongst the Injuns
  a mountain man can keep on livin' free.
I've got my Hawken rifle
  an' even if there ain't no beaver left to trap,
  I reckon I'll be welcome in the lodges o' the 'Rapaho,
  makin' winter meat an' fightin' off the Crow
  an' growin' up that son o' mine
  an' livin' out my time with men
  who know the worth o' bein' free,
  until the day we're all rubbed out
  an' we return to Mother Earth again.

                      ﾠ   ﾠ   ﾠ

Afterword

I reckon this is the place to ask what lesson do we learn from this, if any? Although this book was written to amuse and entertain first its listeners, then its readers, I hope that it also conveys some of the flavor and spirit of the men who made the Rocky Mountain beaver trade happen. They were a rough bunch. Admittedly most of them were initially motivated by greed for the profits to be gained from harvesting valuable beaver pelts; and most maintained a broad streak of renegade disregard for the laws and conventions of civilized society.

Taken as a whole, they were a compendium of social flaws, but we also know of certain virtues displayed by individuals — the piety of Jedediah Smith, the tough but democratic leadership of Jim Bridger and Tom Fitzpatrick, Joe Meek's humor and generosity, and Jim Clyman's thoughtful observations, to name just a few. The courage, fortitude, and resourcefulness of men such as Bill Williams, unlikeable as some might have found Old Solitaire to be, were essential qualities for anybody who intended to survive in the Rockies at that time.

I submit that humor, too, was an important ingredient in the mountain man's make-up. Anyone who has spent time in a foxhole knows the value of humor in an unfunny situation. It can be an effective antidote to terror. And retelling a terrifying experience in humorous, truth-stretching terms can save one a lot of bad dreams.

Mountain men certainly didn't invent the tall tale. They were merely carrying on a tradition that stretches back to antiquity, but they approached the job with a relish and enthusiasm possibly never equalled before or since. The Rockies provided plenty of previously-unknown grist for the story-telling mill and audacious liars were encouraged by an audience renewed each year by fresh recruits to the trapper's trade, greenhorns from the settlements who accompanied the traders to rendezvous, and in the later years, settlers moving to Oregon.

It is a matter of regret that not many of the original tall tales told by mountain men have survived. A few of Jim Bridger's yarns were recorded by Army officers in their journals and were preserved, but most of the best have been lost. It's a pity that Washington Irving didn't write down the outrageous fibs of the mountain men while he was celebrating the exploits and triumphs of the American Fur Company. Imagine the treasury of genial mendacity we might have inherited from the creator of Ichabod Crane, if only he had listened and passed on to us the tall stories of men such as Black Harris, Jim Bridger, and Joe Meek, when they were in their cups at rendezvous and competing with their peers. Instead Irving faithfully discharged his duties as John Jacob Astor's scribbling minion and thereby managed to deprive us of a wealth of American mythology.

Mythology is not frivolous. It is an essential ingredient in the formation of national character. Historical figures are not enough; they are too easily chopped off at the knees by a jealous populace and later by nosey historians.

Brian Boru is impervious to the character assassination suffered by Charles Parnell. Wellington never enjoyed the adulation accorded to King Arthur and his doughty knights of the Round Table. El Cid will never give way to the likes of Francisco Franco and Roland's place in the hearts of Frenchmen is forever safe from the claims of Charles DeGaulle. Siegfried will continue to inspire Germans; and Scots will hopefully forever rally to the cries for freedom uttered by William Wallace and Rob Roy.

The American Myth is of course much less shrouded in the mists of antiquity than its European counterparts. It devolves mostly around the American Cowboy, whose Golden Age enjoyed just about the same life-span as that of the Mountain Man, twenty years, from the late 1860's, when drovers began pushing Texas trail herds north to

Kansas railheads and then on to Wyoming and Montana, to the late 1880's, when ranching became more of a chore than a romantic adventure. Fact is, trail-herding and ranch work was always a dirty, underpaid, dangerous, generally miserable occupation, but glamorized reports of it captured the imagination of Americans who lived in places remote from the day-to-day reality of pushing recalcitrant longhorns northward and tending the livestock of wealthy English and Scottish land barons, many of whom never saw their vast holdings in far-off America.

From the free-flowing pens of penny-awful scribblers such as Ned Buntline emerged a composite portrait of the American Cowboy, strong and silent, honest, generous, firm but fair, courageous, clean-minded, adventurous, a respecter and protector of white womanhood, a sometime-Indian Fighter, and an implacable foe of cattle rustlers, tinhorn gamblers, and other frontier trash. It was just such a picture that drew Charlie Russell to Montana to perform the chores of a horse-wrangler before he began to draw what he saw around him; and it lured Frederic Remington west to sketch and paint what was left of the vanishing West. But the longer these perceptive artists stayed among actual cowboys, the more they became aware of the existence of a family tree.

They began to realize that the cowboy was the lineal descendant of the mountain man, that embodied in the persona of the cowpuncher was his legendary grandfather, the colorful, determined, courageous, free-spirited, lawless, rollicking adventurer who first came to the mountains and prairies of the West, when the frontier was still located on the eastern bank of the Mississippi.

The Mountain Man is truly the bedrock of the essential American Myth, the progenitor of the American Cowboy, and we owe much of our image of him to the pencils, pens, and brushes of Remington and Russell, who perceived in him the spirit that motivates our admiration for the livestock tender of song and legend. Much of that spirit had been lost by the time the cowboy came into being, for what free-trapping mountain man would have been content to spend his lifetime looking after another man's cattle?

Two qualities are rarely encountered among historians, spirit and humor. Admirable as they are, and there have been several excellent chroniclers of the American fur trade, they must be concerned with names, dates, places, events both immediate and remote, underlying economic factors, social phenomena, and whatever other dry and dusty data that enables them to piece together what happened before the current generation arrived. Spirit and humor fall by the wayside, but without those two elements much of what we know of our history could never have occurred.

It was spirit well-furnished with greed that prompted William Ashley and Andrew Henry to assemble their original trapping brigade to ascend the Missouri River and penetrate the beaver-rich Rocky Mountains in 1822. And it was humor that cushioned their men against the perils and hardships of their chosen trade. Their camaraderie was leavened with the yeast of humorous story-telling and laced with an infectious dare-devil spirit that convinced them that they were well-nigh invincible, no matter what Nature and hostile Indians might offer to deter them.

What a pity it is that Washington Irving did not capture for us the stories the mountain men told around their campfires in winter camp and at the annual fur-trading rendezvous. The author of Rip Van Winkle and the The Legend of Sleepy Hollow certainly would have enjoyed those outrageous lies. If only he had taken up his creative quill as well as the pedestrian pencil of a contemporary historian of a commercial venture, he could have put Ned Buntline and his ilk to shame.

While I'm wishing, I wish, too, that William Drummond Stewart could have taken Charlie Russell to rendezvous in 1835, instead of Alfred Jacob Miller, a talented painter and watercolorist, to be sure, but a shade too sober for the doin's that surrounded him there. Charlie would have caught the spirit and the humor of that rollicking rendezvous and our culture would be wealthier because of it.

As it is, we have only fragments and broken shards from which to reconstruct what occurred at that time. It's a worthwhile chore, however, for we have lost much of the spirit that motivated the men who pursued the beaver trade. We have grown crabby and inward-looking, untrusting of our fellows and our environment, as any overly-urbanized people is likely to become. And although the experience must be vicarious I believe that revisiting that time and place and the men who gave it life and substance, in whatever form is available — art, literature, reenactments — is beneficial to ourselves and our national culture.

Here is one way that some people have chosen to achieve that end. During the last roughly 40 years there has developed a rapidly-growing recreational activity called buckskinning or sometimes simply rendezvous, not only in the United States but in Canada and several Western European countries as well.

Rendezvous seeks to recreate a typical rendezvous encampment of the 1820's and '30's, complete in every possible visual detail — clothing, shelter, cooking implements, general camp gear, and weapons such as muzzleloading firearms, tomahawks, and knives. No Coleman stoves or lanterns. Necessary modern conveniences such as ice chests and water containers are concealed in boxes or stowed inside tipis and tents of a design and material appropriate to the period. Cooking is done over a campfire. Music is totally acoustic and story-telling is encouraged.

Unlike many military reenactment groups, rendezvous is a family affair. Men, women, and children participate enthusiastically, in their respective camps and in organized activities, such as blackpowder shooting contests, knife- and tomahawk-throwing, fryingpan-tosses, story-telling often called liars' contests, music and sing-alongs, and races afoot and horseback. Buckskinners range in age from toddlers and newborns to nonegenarians, each doing what he enjoys, and sometimes simply not much at all.

Traders' Row is an important element in modern rendezvous, as it was in 1820's and '30's, for it is here, housed in white canvas tents and marquees, that goods that could have been available before 1840 are offered for sale — beads and beadwork, feathers, clothing, textiles, leather, sinew, tools and utensils, books, pottery, enamelware, and glassware, flintlock and percussion firearms, knives, horse gear, foodstuffs both prepared and in bulk, primitive toys, and a vast variety of whatever a trader thinks might attract the eye and purse of a customer. Modern products are forbidden. Buckskinners flock to replenish supplies required for winter craft projects for next year's rendezvous and to equip their camp with ever more authentic furnishings and utensils.

When a newcomer first arrives at a large rendezvous he beholds a sight much like that which the Israelites might have seen the morning after they were blessed with manna — a landscape dotted with white canvas shelters of nearly every description — tipis, Baker and wall tents, marquees, pyramids, lean-tos, diamond flies, wickiups and rude brush shelters — stretching far and wide across a meadow or plain and disappearing into the trees. It's breath-taking and beautiful. And as he strolls among the camps he might, if he squints just a little, suppose himself to be carried back in time to the wilderness of the 1830's.

Parking lots, by the way, are tucked away out of sight, behind a nearby hill or grove of trees.

I've tried to describe here what modern rendezvous is; now it's important to say what it ain't. It's not political, religious, racial, paramilitary, or dedicated to anything other than good-natured people getting together in the outdoors for a weekend or as long as two weeks to get in touch with their historic, cultural, and natural roots. One of my favorite recollections concerns one time that I arrived at a rendezvous and saw at the registration booth a battered and broken old pack-basket which bore a sign which proclaimed: "Leave your political, religious, social, and racial opinions here. You can pick them up on your way out, if you still want 'em."

Rendezvous is not a closed society. Everybody's welcome. Fact is, buckskinners appear to suffer from an endemic disease, proselytizing.

They are constantly trying to convince their friends and neighbors and even strangers to get interested in their activity. And when a newcomer shows up at a primitive rendezvous (appropriately garbed in pre-1840 clothing, I should mention) he will very likely be deluged with help, advice, and often gifts of extra clothing and camp gear.

It's appropriate to mention, too, the matter of firearms. Blackpowder shooting is an important part of rendezvous for many, but not all, buckskinners. Honing their skill with flintlock or percussion muzzleloading rifles, pistols, and fowling pieces, even home-made cannons — shooting at targets, never critters — is a pleasurable recreation for many buckskinners, but it is certainly not required. No modern (later than 1840 design) firearms are allowed at rendezvous and every individual in camp enforces safety rules. Rendezvous is not a gun-owners' convention, by any means, and most buckskinner gatherings are not affiliated with any central organization and have no continuing executive group. Officers (booshways) are elected each year by the participants to organize and run the rendezvous which will take place a year or two hence. Fact is, two-thirds of the nine large annual American regional rendezvous recently seceded from the National Muzzle Loading Rifle Association, mainly because they resented any central control of their activities. Free-trapping mountain men didn't take kindly to authority and neither do modern-day buckskinners.

My purpose here is not to describe the history and precise local character of modern rendezvous, except to say that local participants tend to reflect in some degree the aspects of significant American history which took place in their particular area of the United States. Thus eastern groups for the most part gravitate toward re-creating the appearance of longhunters and colonial militia, while Midwestern, Rocky Mountain, and West Coast participants are more likely to emulate the Rocky Mountain beaver-trappers and traders in matters of clothing and shelter.

Rendezvous aficionados of the Southwest tend to reflect the Mexican clothing styles that one might have seen in the streets of Taos and Santa Fe during the heyday of the beaver trade.

The year 1840, however, is the cut-off date for most, if not all, such groups. The beginning date is much more loosely applied. The Rocky Mountain, Pacific Coast, and Southwest people usually bracket their period between the years 1820 and 1840, the time of extensive beaver-trapping in the Rockies. Eastern groups generally prefer an earlier starting date, which encompasses longhunters and Colonial militia and thus permits an expansion of permissible clothing styles. Rocky Mountain garb favors buckskins — breechclouts and leggin's for those courageous enough to wear them — woolens, and calicos, generally emulating the mountain man's highest sartorial compliment, "I took ye for an Injun."

Women at western rendezvous tend to wear squaw dresses made of buckskin or wool — often elaborately decorated with beadwork, quillwork, shells, elk teeth, or dew claws — or simple calico for camp chores and strenuous activities. Those who don't choose to dress in Indian style generally wear clothing appropriate to frontier women of the period, although variations of those designs are considerable.

Barbers most likely would disapprove of buckskinning if they knew about it, for many dedicated male buckskinners let their hair grow long year-round, year after year, emulating the mountain men, most of whom never cut their hair. Beards, however, are probably more plentiful nowadays than they were in the Rockies during the glory days of the fur trade, for Indian women were not fond of facial hair on their white-eyes suitors. Their contemporary sisters seem not to mind it, at least not quite as much.

That more or less describes the who, what, where, and how of rendezvous; the why of it is more difficult to define. There is certainly a strong element of retreating into Fantasyland, into a bygone time when we suppose that values were straightforward and people felt that they could better control their surroundings. For many, rendezvous is a temporary rejection of here and now and a world which has come to baffle their imagination, a renewal of simple values and a return to the camaraderie we prized so highly when we were very young.

Social and economic distinctions well-nigh disappear at rendezvous. White collars and blue fade into buckskin and a man's skill as a gunsmith or a musician is admired far more than his elevation on the corporate ladder. Fact is, he's not likely to mention or inquire about such matters.

So it is that the myth and the spirit of the mountain man continues to strengthen the backbone of American culture, not only among buckskinners but also in the hearts and unconscious minds of city-dwellers who never heard of Jim Bridger and Joe Meek and couldn't care less if they had. Those greedy, dirty, ragged, resolute, dissolute, freedom-loving beaver trappers, who laughed at danger because it was better than crying about it and who sired the American Cowboy, managed to put their indelible stamp on the American character. And we're all better off because of it.

                ô   ô   ô

Glossary

This glossary has been included to explain some of the words and terms used in this book which may not be readily discoverable in standard dictionaries. It is no doubt incomplete, but it attempts to make it easier for the reader to understand some of the unfamiliar words and references used in the stories.

Absaroka *n* A Crow Indian. The Crows, although a numerous and warlike Indian nation, were generally disposed to be friendly with white trappers, preferring to trade with them and to steal their livestock and other possessions rather than taking their scalps. Also (pl), a mountain range in what is now south central Montana. *Also sometimes spelled* **Absarokee, Absorkee**, *etc.*

Aitch-bee-cee *n* HBC, the British-owned Hudson's Bay Company, which dominated the Canadian and northwestern fur trade until Americans challenged its domain in the 1820's. Also interpreted as Here Before Christ.

apishamore *n* An ornamental saddle blanket, frequently embroidered with porcupine quillwork or beadwork.

apple pie *n* As the term is used in these stories, apple cider flavored with pie spices such as cinnamon and nutmeg and laced with grain alcohol.

bacon-eater *n* This term is translated literally from the French term mangeur de lard, which was applied to just about anyone in the mountains who was not considered to be a proper mountaineer. In other words, a pilgrim, greenhorn, or tenderfoot.

Beckwith *n* James P. Beckwourth, a much-publicized mulatto mountain man and sometime Crow war chief, whose real and imagined exploits during the beaver trade era were flamboyantly chronicled in an 1856 biography written by T.D. Bonner, a book remarkable for its bombast and stilted language worthy of a sideshow barker. Beckwourth, as he preferred to be called in later life, was generally known among his trapping companions as Jim Beckwith, which is why I have used that spelling in these stories.

Big-belly *n* An Atsina Indian, variously called Gros Ventres, Grovants, and Prairie Blackfeet. Although they were at times closely allied with certain tribes of the Blackfoot Nation, they are not of that people. Most mountain men did not, however, make that distinction. The French term Gros ventre literally means Big-belly and was apparently derived from a predilection of members of that group to drop in on their neighbors and eat them out of house and home and then to bid them a fond farewell, until next time.

Bloods *n pl* Members of the Kainah tribe, one of the three principal tribes of the Blackfoot nation.

booshway *n* An American corruption of the French word *bourgeois*, which was used to designate either a principal trader or the leader of a trapping brigade, who was also called a *partisan*, a term which I have not used in any of these stories.

bourgeois *n* See *booshway* above.

cap *n* Percussion cap. A tiny brass cylinder containing a small explosive charge designed to ignite and explode the principal charge of gunpowder in a muzzleloading firearm. Percussion rifles became the state-of-the-art weapon during the latter half of the beaver trade era, 1820-40, although many mountain men resisted that innovation, preferring their flintlock rifles, which required only gunpowder, lead, and readily-available flints. Percussion caps had to be transported to the mountains by rendezvous traders; but then, so did powder and lead.

cordelle *n* A rope used to haul a keelboat upstream when sail, poling, or rowing proved inadequate for the task. Several men would be detailed to walk along the bank or through shallow water, pulling on the *cordelle*, which was attached to the mast of the keelboat, until other means permitted the craft to proceed upstream.

engagé *n* A French word used to describe what was usually a French-Canadian camp helper, customarily detailed to perform chores such as cooking, gathering firewood, fleshing and stretching beaver pelts, and similar menial, non-trapping tasks.

Ephraim *n* Usually, *Old Ephraim*, a familiar term among mountain men for grizzly bears, applied equally to boars and sows.

frizzen *n* That portion of the lock of a flintlock firearm against which the flint strikes when the hammer falls, scraping off a tiny flake of iron and creating sparks, which ignite the priming gunpowder, which explodes and travels through the touch hole and ignites the main propulsive charge of the weapon.

Grayback *n* The common louse, with which both Redman and white were much afflicted during the Fur Trade Era. Also, a term of opprobrium applied by mountain men to flatlanders, specifically farmers.

Grovant *n* See *Big-belly* above.

hivernant *n* A mountain man who had spent at least one winter in the Rocky Mountains, which qualified him to claim veteran status among his comrades. The word is derived from the French word *hiver* (winter).

Kah-ee-nah *n* See *Kainah* below.

Kainah *n* One of the three principal tribes of the Blackfoot Nation, often called *Bloods*.

Lahcotah or **Lakota** *n* Proper name of a principal branch of the Sioux Nation, which is comprised of many tribes, such as Oglala, Hunkpapa, Teton, Yanktonnais, Sans Arcs, etc.

medicine *n* In the sense that it is used in these stories, medicine refers to an object or occurrence that possesses or portends supernatural power for either good or evil (good medicine or bad medicine), according to North American Plains Indian beliefs.

metheglin *n* An alcoholic beverage made of fermented honey, malt, yeast, and water (mead), customarily laced with grain alcohol at fur-trading rendezvous and similar festive occasions in the Rocky Mountains.

mover *n* A term applied by mountain men to settlers traveling west to Oregon or California.

Nor'west *n* or Nor'wester, an employee of the British-owned Northwest Fur Company. Although that company merged with the Hudson's Bay Company in 1821, many mountain men continued to refer to their British and Canadian rivals as Nor'westers.

paloosie *n* Corruption of appaloosa, a hardy breed of horses developed by the Nez Percé Indians, generally characterized by a distinctively spotted hide, ratty mane and tail, scolera, striated hoofs, and a distinctive conformation.

pan *n* That portion of the lock of a flintlock firearm which holds the priming gunpowder, which, when exposed to sparks generated by the flint and the frizzen (see *frizzen* above) explodes and ignites the main propulsive charge.

Piegan *n* Common Americanized name of the *Pikuni* tribe, one of the three principal tribes of the Blackfoot Nation.

Pikuni *n* Proper name of one of the three principal tribes of the Blackfoot Nation. See *Piegan* above.

plew *n* Corruption of the French word plus, a slang term among French-Canadian and American trappers and traders denoting a beaver pelt, referring to its value.

plunder *n* A general word used by mountain men when referring to their possessions.

poredevil *n* A slang term employed by mountain men to describe an outcast Indian, usually one who had committed a transgression serious enough to warrant his expulsion from his band, tribe, and nation. No other tribe would take him in, so a poredevil was forced to wander alone and friendless in the wilderness. **Syn.** EXILE, OUTCAST, PARIAH, UNWELCOME PERSON.

possibles *n* A general word used by mountain men to describe their possessions, usually specifically those carried on their person or on their saddle horse.

priming *n* The gunpowder which ignites the main propulsive charge in a flintlock firearm. See *pan* and *frizzen* above.

Rocky Mountain College *n* A facetious term among mountain men which referred to winter camp, when the weather was too cold for beaver-trapping and where many men, Joe Meek among them, learned to read and write. Those who could read and who possessed a book or two would often read aloud to their illiterate comrades. Shakespeare and Sir Walter Scott were among their favorite authors, together with whoever wrote the Bible.

Sassenach *n* A Gaelic word which means *foreigner*, *outlander*, or *enemy*, specifically applied by the Scots and the Irish to the English, who certainly fit all of those definitions. Not always capitalized and usually opprobrious.

Siksika *n* One of the three principal tribes of the Blackfoot Nation. The Siksika are often referred to as *Proper Blackfeet*.

Touse *n* Taos, a city in what is now the State of New Mexico, a favorite wintering hang-out for many mountain men, especially those who worked the beaver streams of the southern Rockies.

trade gun *n* Smoothbore musket, usually a flintlock and frequently of inferior manufacture, commonly used as a trade item with Indians during the early 1800's. Flintlock muskets were generally preferred by the Indians because they required neither percussion caps (see cap above) nor precisely-calibrated lead balls.

Wakan-ton-ka *n* Lahcotah (Sioux) proper noun meaning Great Spirit, Supreme Being, Creator of the Universe.

Waugh! Evidently a common exclamation among mountain men, supposedly derived from the grunting of a grizzly bear. We have as authorities for the existence of this exclamatory remark the writings of Lewis Garrard, an Ohio tourist, and George Frederick Ruxton, an English adventurer, each of whom spent considerable time with the few remaining mountain men, Old Bill Williams among them, in the southern Rockies in the 1840's.

                 ❧   ❧   ❧

About the Author

Edward Louis Henry (a.k.a. Poredevil) has been a working cowhand, rodeo contestant and Wild West performer, WWII infantry sergeant (Pacific), newspaper reporter, U.S. Foreign Service officer, and executive speechwriter, plus has spent thirty years in advertising. A lifelong horseman and outdoorsman, Henry is active in mountain man rendezvous. Western history is his abiding passion. Henry is a member of Western Writers of America and is the author of the Temple Buck Quartet and Poredevil's Beaver Tales.

Other books by Edward Louis Henry

THE TEMPLE BUCK QUARTET
A Rocky Mountain Odyssey, 1822-1837

Volume I: Backbone of the World, 1822–1824 is a coming-of-age story of the first two years of the Rocky Mountain fur trade, 1822-24. It is told in his own words by Temple Buck, an Ohio-born lad whose rollicking tale begins with growing up in the Ohio wilderness, how he is kidnapped aboard evil Mike Fink's keelboat, is rescued by a beautiful St. Louis madam, and finally enlists in Ashley and Henry's first expedition up the Missouri River to the beaver-rich Rockies and a wealth of adventure and undreamed-of new experiences. This painstakingly researched tale blends historical and fictional characters in a colorful tapestry of actual events spiced with bloody battles, Indian customs and characters, homespun humor, and earthy romance. If you've ever wished for absolute freedom and hair-raising adventure in the early Old West, come along with Temple and his trapper companions and breathe the free, pure air of the Rocky Mountains!

Volume II: Free Men, 1824–1826 chronicles the exploits of Temple Buck and his rowdy trapper companions in the American Rocky Mountain fur trade from 1824-1826. In this, the second volume of the Temple Buck Quartet, they push ever farther west in their quest for beaver pelts, exploring new country and encountering fresh adventures, some of them welcome, others not at all. This well-researched tale, told in Temple's own words, blends historical and fictional characters against a colorful backdrop of actual events, pungently flavored with gory battles with hostile Indians, homespun humor, and earthy romance, culminating in Temple's disappointing return to his Ohio birthplace.

Volume III: Shinin' Times!, 1828–1833 Temple Buck returns to the Rockies, rejoining his trapping bunch and picking up the free, unfettered life of the American free trapper where he left off in 1826. He and the other members of his trapping bunch explore uncharted new country and gain new and different experience in a changing and expanding fur trade. Their personal lives change, as well, as they take on new responsibilities while continuing to enjoy the happy-go-lucky life of the Rocky Mountain free trapper, its rich flavor much improved now by their wider knowledge, deeper experience, and greater appreciation of everything that living in the American wilderness can provide for men who possess the the savvy and smarts and courage to survive on Nature's bosom.

Volume IV: Glory Days Gone Under, 1834–1837, is the fourth and final volume of the Temple Buck Quartet. All things, good and bad, come to an end. Fashions change and human greed injures even all-bountiful Nature. Faraway factors in Europe and the American East destroyed the market for beaver pelts, which occurred just when beaver were growing scarce in the mountains. Without a market, pelts were worthless. The mountaineer's income was wiped out. White settlers, following trails blazed by the early trappers, were moving west, bringing with them families, farming, civilized customs, laws, and missionaries, all of which the trappers despised, corrupting the Indians and crowding them off their ancestral lands, all in the name of a Manifest Destiny that mountaineers, tough, resourceful, and courageous as they were, were powerless to resist.

Poredevil's Beaver Tales You can almost hear the voice of a tough, experienced early 19th century mountain man in this collection of 24 humorous mountain man tall stories and poems narrated in a loose sort of verse. All of the stories contain glimpses of the difficult and dangerous life of that rowdy breed of men who challenged America's uncharted wilderness and who survived and triumphed because of their courage, fortitude and unquenchable laughter in the face of hardship and peril.

For more information on these and other great books, visit
http//christophermatthewspub.com.

CPSIA information can be obtained at www.ICGtesting.com
Printed in the USA
BVOW040727191211

278629BV00001B/9/P

9 780983 722564